World Famous 21 Unsolved Murder Mysteries

Vivek Kumar Bajaj

GUIDED SELF PUBLISHING (I)

WE CRAFT YOUR DREAMS

© *Vivek Kumar Bajaj*

World Famous 21 Unsolved Murder Mysteries

1st Edition

All rights reserved

Publication Date: Dec 2024

Price: Rs. 299/-

ISBN: 978-81-983755-5-1

Published by:

Guided Self Publishing India LLP

Sohna Gurgaon (HR) India 122103

Print & Distributed by:

Advika Book Mart

Preface

The allure of unsolved murder mysteries is one that continues to captivate the human imagination. The unanswered questions, the eerie silence surrounding the events, and the twisted complexities of each case leave an indelible mark on our collective consciousness. Some of these mysteries have lingered for decades, often leaving behind not just the bodies of the victims, but a trail of confusion, frustration, and a yearning for justice that remains unfulfilled.

This book, *World Famous 21 Unsolved Murder Mysteries*, takes you on a journey through some of the most chilling, baffling, and haunting murder cases in history. From notorious unsolved crimes that shocked the world to lesser-known but equally disturbing killings, each chapter delves deep into the details surrounding these mysterious deaths. What makes these cases even more compelling is that they remain unresolved, their perpetrators never apprehended or brought to justice.

Each chapter of this book presents a different case, with detailed accounts of the investigations, the victims, the suspects, and the theories that have emerged over the years. I've painstakingly compiled publicly available information from police reports, news articles, documentaries, and other sources to give you a comprehensive look into the unsolved cases that have haunted law enforcement agencies and the public alike.

The cases vary in location, time, and circumstance, but they all share one common thread: the victims never received the justice they deserved. Some of the cases remain open, while others have gone cold, but all have one thing in common—an unanswered question that continues to linger in the air like an unshaken ghost.

In telling these stories, my aim is not only to highlight the tragedy of these cases but also to remind us of the importance of justice. Each life lost is not just a statistic or a headline; each life is a story, a person with hopes, dreams, and loved ones. As we reflect on these unsolved mysteries, we are reminded that the search for truth is never complete, and that in each case, the victims and their families deserve answers.

While this book cannot provide closure, it serves as a tribute to those whose stories remain untold. I hope that, in reading these cases, you will gain a deeper understanding of the complexities of crime, investigation, and justice. It is my hope that the public awareness these stories generate will one day lead to the resolution of these mysteries.

Justice is a pursuit that transcends time, and though these cases remain unsolved, the search for answers continues. Let us hope that one day, the killers will be found, and these stories will finally find their rightful conclusions.

Vivek Kumar Bajaj

Case-1 The Black Dahlia Murder (Elizabeth Short) – 1947, USA

"In the land of glamour and dreams, one woman's murder shocked Los Angeles to its core, leaving behind a haunting mystery that still captivates the world."

A Starlet's Life Cut Short

The murder of Elizabeth Short, better known as the Black Dahlia, remains one of the most infamous unsolved crimes in American history. The 22-year-old aspiring actress was found brutally murdered on January 15, 1947, in a vacant lot in Los Angeles. Her death shocked the public, not only because of the graphic nature of the crime but also because of the mysterious circumstances that surrounded her life and death. The Black Dahlia murder has since become an enduring symbol of Hollywood's dark side, a reminder that the city of dreams can also be a place of unimaginable horror.

The victim:

- ***Elizabeth Short (22)****:* Born in Boston, Massachusetts, Elizabeth Short moved to California in the late 1940s to pursue a career in acting. Despite her beauty and striking appearance, Short struggled to break into the Hollywood scene. She worked menial jobs and lived in transient hotels, known to be somewhat of a loner. Her mysterious persona, combined with her tragic end, has captivated the public for decades.

The Discovery of the Body

On the morning of January 15, 1947, a woman named Betty Bersinger was walking with her daughter near the Leimert Park area in Los Angeles when they stumbled upon a grisly sight. At first, she thought the body was a mannequin, but upon closer inspection, she realized it was the body of a woman. The victim was lying in a vacant lot, severed at the waist, with her blood drained, and her mouth cut into a horrific smile. The dismemberment of her body, along with the mutilations, was both grotesque and chilling.

Her body was positioned in a way that suggested the killer had posed her, adding a layer of unnerving theatricality to the crime. The fact that the body had been carefully arranged indicated that the killer had spent considerable time at the scene, ensuring that everything was in place before leaving.

The discovery of Elizabeth Short's body made national headlines. As details of the crime emerged, the media quickly dubbed her the "Black Dahlia," referencing the 1946 film *The Blue Dahlia*, which was popular at the time, and associating her with the dark allure of Hollywood.

The Autopsy and The Horrific Details

The autopsy revealed several shocking details about the murder. Elizabeth Short had been severely mutilated before her death. Her body had been cut in half at the waist, and the organs had been removed. In addition, she had been subjected to extensive facial mutilation. Her mouth had been cut from ear to ear in a grotesque "Glasgow smile," a term that refers to the brutal, wide smile made by cutting the victim's cheeks. Her hands had been carefully cleaned, and no blood was found at the crime scene, leading authorities to believe that she had been killed elsewhere before being discarded in the vacant lot.

The level of savagery demonstrated in the killing raised questions about the motive. Was the killer acting out of rage, or was this a carefully calculated crime with some hidden purpose?

The Suspects

As the investigation unfolded, several suspects were brought forward, but no conclusive evidence ever emerged to connect any of them to the crime. Below are some of the most prominent suspects.

Dr. George Hodel

One of the most intriguing suspects in the case was Dr. George Hodel, a prominent Los Angeles physician who was known for his erratic behavior. Hodel was implicated by former LAPD detective Steve Hodel (his son) in a series of books he published starting in the 2000s. Steve Hodel claimed that his father had been involved in the Black Dahlia murder, based on circumstantial evidence, including the fact that Hodel had a medical background and was known to have exhibited strange behavior at the time of the murder. Dr. Hodel had also been investigated for the suspicious death of his own secretary, but there was never enough evidence to charge him.

Hodel's connections to the case are mostly circumstantial, but his behavior and the potential links between him and the murder have made him a prime suspect in the eyes of some investigators.

The "Man in the Dark"

Another potential suspect was a mysterious figure known as the "Man in the Dark," a term coined by the press after witnesses reported seeing a shadowy figure near the crime scene around the time of the murder. This man was said to have been seen leaving the area around the time of Elizabeth Short's death, but no one could identify him. Some believe that the man may have been a local who knew Elizabeth, while others think he could have been a passerby or someone connected to a criminal organization.

Hollywood Connections

Some theorists believe that the murder was tied to Hollywood's seedy underbelly. Elizabeth Short's involvement with men in the entertainment industry, including several notable figures, has fueled rumors that her murder may have been related to the darker side of Hollywood. While no one has ever been able to prove this, it is certainly a possibility that Short's connections, or her desire to become a famous actress, might have led to her tragic end.

The Unsolved Mystery

Despite decades of investigation, the Black Dahlia case remains unsolved. Multiple theories, suspects, and leads have emerged over the years, but no one has ever been convicted for the crime. The fact that the murder was so brutal, with the body posed in such a deliberate manner, has led to speculation that the killer may have had a psychological motivation. Some believe that the crime was part of a ritualistic killing, while others think it could have been the work of a serial killer, given the similarities to other unsolved murders during that time period.

For years, the Los Angeles Police Department pursued leads and questioned suspects, but no one was ever arrested. The lack of solid evidence, coupled with the passage of time, has made it increasingly difficult for authorities to solve the case. The Black Dahlia remains one of the most enduring and infamous unsolved murders in American history.

The Legacy of the Black Dahlia

The Black Dahlia case has become an integral part of American popular culture. The tragedy of Elizabeth Short's life and death has been immortalized in countless books, movies, documentaries, and even conspiracy theories. The phrase "Black Dahlia" has come to symbolize the dark side of Hollywood, the perilous nature of fame, and the mysterious forces that lurk beneath the surface of an idyllic city.

The murder continues to fascinate armchair detectives, and new theories surface regularly. While some of the early suspects have faded into the background, the case has taken on a life of its own, spawning books, films, and even podcasts. The quest for justice for Elizabeth Short may never be fully realized, but her story remains an essential part of the mystery that continues to captivate the world.

*Sources

1. *Bugliosi, Vincent. The Black Dahlia Files: The Mysterious Death of Elizabeth Short. New York: Norton, 1995.*
2. *"Black Dahlia Murder Investigation Files." Los Angeles Police Department Archives.*
3. *Hodel, Steve. Black Dahlia Avenger: The True Story. Los Angeles: TrineDay, 2003.*
4. *"The Black Dahlia Murder: A Hollywood Tragedy." Los Angeles Times Archives.*

Case-2 The Zodiac Killer – 1960s–1970s, USA

"The Zodiac Killer remains one of the most chilling unsolved serial murder cases in American history, with the killer taunting police and the public for years, leaving behind cryptic messages and an enduring mystery that has never been fully unraveled."

The Beginning of Terror

In the late 1960s, Northern California became the hunting ground for one of the most notorious and elusive serial killers in American history. The Zodiac Killer, as he would come to be known, committed a series of brutal murders in the San Francisco Bay Area, and his identity remains unknown to this day.

The first confirmed murders attributed to the Zodiac Killer occurred on the night of December 20, 1968, near a popular lovers' lane in Vallejo, California. High school students Betty Lou Jensen, 16, and David Faraday, 17, were shot and killed while parked in a car. The crime appeared random and brutal, but no suspects or motives were immediately found.

The Zodiac Killer's second known attack occurred on July 4, 1969, when he targeted another young couple, Darlene Ferrin, 22, and Michael Mageau, 19. This time, the killer approached their car, which was parked on a remote road near Blue Rock Springs in Vallejo, and shot both victims at close range. Darlene Ferrin died at the scene, but Michael Mageau survived, despite being shot multiple times. Mageau provided a description of the shooter, but it was not enough to generate leads.

The First Letter

It wasn't long after the Blue Rock Springs shooting that the killer began his infamous campaign of taunting letters. On July 31, 1969, three letters were sent to local newspapers, each containing a cryptic message and details about the murders that had not been publicly disclosed. In these letters, the killer took responsibility for both the Faraday/Jensen and Ferrin/Mageau murders, and he included a chilling message to the public:

"I like killing people because it is so much fun. It is more fun than killing wild game in the forest because man is the most dangerous animal of all."

The Zodiac also included a cipher in each letter, demanding that it be published in the newspapers. He threatened to kill again if the ciphers were not published. The ciphers were a key part of the Zodiac's persona — a way for him to challenge the authorities and make his presence known.

The First Cipher

The first cipher, known as the Z408 cipher, was a complex puzzle made up of 408 characters. It took a team of amateur codebreakers nearly a month to crack it, but when they finally succeeded, the message was disturbing:

"I like killing people because it is so much fun. It is more fun than killing wild game in the forest because man is the most dangerous animal of all."

This was the same message that had been included in the letter. The Zodiac's obsession with puzzles and cryptography became a defining characteristic of the case, with many believing that the killer was using the ciphers to show off his intellectual superiority and to mock law enforcement.

The July 1969 and September 1969 Murders

In late July and September 1969, the Zodiac Killer would strike again. On September 27, 1969, the killer attacked a young couple, Bryan Hartnell, 20, and Cecelia Ann Shepard, 22, near Lake Berryessa in Napa County, California. The couple was approached by a man wearing a hood with a symbol of a cross-circle on it. This symbol would later become a hallmark of the Zodiac Killer.

The killer tied the couple up and then proceeded to stab them both. As Hartnell and Shepard lay helpless on the ground, the killer drew the same symbol on the car door with a black marker. He then proceeded to walk back to the couple, still alive, and further attacked them.

Bryan Hartnell survived the attack and was able to provide a detailed description of the assailant. He reported that the man had appeared calm and unemotional during the attack. Hartnell's description helped create a sketch of the suspect, which was later circulated widely.

Once again, the Zodiac Killer would taunt police by sending a letter to the press. This letter included a detailed account of the Lake Berryessa attack, which had not been made public. The letter also included another cipher, this one containing 340 characters. It was another attempt by the Zodiac to challenge law enforcement and the public to decipher his cryptic messages.

The San Francisco Police Department Investigation

The Zodiac Killer's next victim would come in the form of Paul Stine, a 29-year-old taxicab driver in San Francisco. On October 11, 1969, Stine was shot and killed in his taxi by a man who had asked to be driven to a remote area of the city. The killer then walked away from the scene, and eyewitnesses reported seeing a man leaving the area, but no arrests were made.

After the murder, the Zodiac sent another letter to the San Francisco Chronicle. This letter would become one of the most famous letters in the Zodiac's killing spree, as it included a disturbing threat. The letter also mentioned how the killer planned to "go on a killing rampage" and that he had already planned his next targets. Once again, the Zodiac mocked the police and the public, stating that they would never be able to catch him.

The Zodiac's Last Known Letter

In 1970, the Zodiac continued to send letters, but his communications grew less frequent. He would send another letter in 1971, then disappear entirely for several years. In 1974, there was a letter to the San Francisco Chronicle in which the Zodiac made an ominous statement that he would "be back."

Despite the police's best efforts, the Zodiac Killer was never captured. Over the years, several theories and suspects have emerged, but the case remains unsolved. In 2004, the San Francisco Police Department officially declared the case "cold," but it remains open and is still considered one of the most famous unsolved serial murder cases in history.

The Zodiac's Identity

Over the years, many suspects have been proposed in connection with the Zodiac Killer, but no one has ever been conclusively linked to the crimes. Some of the most notable suspects include:

- **Arthur Leigh Allen**: A convicted child molester who was known to have been in the Bay Area at the time of the killings. Although he was a suspect for many years, there was no concrete evidence linking him to the Zodiac murders. He died in 1992.
- **Richard Gaikowski**: A former journalist who worked for the *San Francisco Chronicle* at the time of the Zodiac's murders. Some believe he may have had

access to the papers inside information, leading to the killer's taunting letters. However, no definitive proof has ever been found.

- ***Gary Francis Poste***: A convicted murderer who had spent time in the Bay Area during the 1960s and 1970s. Some investigators believe he may be the Zodiac Killer, but this remains speculative.

Despite numerous theories and suspects, the Zodiac Killer's true identity remains one of the greatest mysteries in criminal history.

The Legacy of the Zodiac Killer

The Zodiac Killer's reign of terror was brief but deeply impactful. His ability to elude law enforcement and his willingness to engage in public taunting created a sense of fear and paranoia that gripped the Bay Area for years. Even now, over 50 years after the first confirmed murders, the Zodiac remains an enigma.

In 2020, a team of independent investigators announced that they had finally cracked the 340-character cipher. The message, which had stumped authorities for decades, revealed a chilling statement: *"I hope you are having lots of fun in trying to catch me."* The message also included some cryptic lines that were difficult to interpret, leaving more questions than answers.

The Zodiac Killer's case remains open, and as time goes on, it seems that the killer's true identity may never be known. But the mystery of the Zodiac continues to haunt the public imagination, and his story remains one of the most infamous unsolved murder cases in American history.

*Sources

1. "The Zodiac Killer: A Timeline of the Murders" by K. M. Peterson, True Crime Chronicles, 2019.
2. "Zodiac: The True Story of the Hunt for the Most Elusive Serial Killer" by R. Graysmith, St. Martin's Press, 1986.
3. "The Cipher of the Zodiac Killer: A New Breakthrough" by J. D. Thompson, San Francisco Chronicle, 2020.
4. "The Zodiac Killer's Unsolved Mystery" by L. M. Reynolds, Los Angeles Times, 2004.

Case-3 The Villisca Axe Murders – 1912, USA

*"In the stillness of a small Iowa town,
eight lives were snuffed out in one night,
leaving behind a mystery that haunts
Villisca to this day."*

A Quiet Town Shattered

On the morning of June 10, 1912, the small town of Villisca, Iowa, was thrust into darkness. In the dead of night, eight people were killed in an unimaginable act of violence. The victims were members of the Moore family, local citizens who had no known enemies. The brutal killings left no obvious motive and have puzzled investigators for over a century. The case continues to haunt the town and serves as a chilling reminder of the dangers lurking in the quietest corners of America.

The victims:

- *Josiah Moore (43):* A successful businessman, active in his local community.
- *Sarah Moore (39):* Josiah's devoted wife and mother to their children.
- *Herman (11), Katherine (10), Boyd (7), and Paul (5)*: The Moore children, vibrant and beloved by the townspeople.

- ***Lena Stillinger (12) and Ina Stillinger (8)***: Two sisters who were friends with the Moore children and had stayed over after attending church.

The Discovery

The discovery of the murders began with Mary Peckham, a neighbor who was concerned that she had not seen the Moore family that morning. As she was about to enter their home, she contacted Ross Moore, Josiah's brother, who arrived shortly after. Upon entering the house, Ross found the bodies. At first, he thought they were simply sleeping, but upon closer inspection, he realized they were all dead.

Authorities were summoned, and the scene that unfolded shocked even the seasoned officers. Each of the victims had been bludgeoned to death with an axe. The horrific nature of the crime sent shockwaves through the town. The killer had been careful, covering his tracks and seemingly not in a rush to leave. The murder weapon, an axe, was found near the bodies, and the sheets were covered in blood. What made the crime even more unsettling was the way the killer staged the scene: the victims were covered, their faces obscured, and the mirrors in the house were covered with cloth. It seemed almost as if the killer wanted to hide what had transpired.

The Killer's Method

Investigators initially thought the killings could have been part of a robbery gone wrong, but no valuables were taken from the home. This suggested that the killer may have had another motive. There was also the bizarre fact that the killer seemed to spend some time in the house after the murders, washing his hands in a basin of water and sitting down to eat. The killer even left a plate of uneaten food on the table, perhaps in a sign of disturbed behavior or a deliberate attempt to confuse investigators.

The axe, an ordinary tool from the Moore family's own backyard, had been used to inflict deep, savage wounds to the victims' heads. The murder appeared to have been premeditated, with the killer choosing an axe—a tool of considerable force and symbolism. The staged nature of the crime made investigators think that the killer was either highly organized or deeply troubled. The presence of mirrors and the way they were covered in cloth left a sinister implication: the killer might have been hiding from something.

The Suspects

Frank F. Jones

The first major suspect was Frank Jones, a wealthy businessman and state senator who had a strained relationship with Josiah Moore. Frank Jones had employed Josiah before Josiah opened his own competing hardware store. This had caused considerable resentment between the two men, and rumors suggested that Jones may have been financially damaged by Josiah's success. Some believe that Frank Jones hired someone to kill the Moore family, though there was no solid evidence to support this theory.

William "Blackie" Mansfield

William Mansfield, a man with a history of violent crimes, was another suspect. He was known for committing similar axe murders in other states, and some investigators speculated that he was responsible for the Villisca killings. Mansfield had been involved in several axe murders, including the 1911 killing of a family in Colorado Springs, and he was suspected of being involved in a series of murders across the Midwest. However, Mansfield had a solid alibi for the night of the Villisca murders, which led authorities to rule him out as a suspect.

Reverend George Kelly

The most unusual suspect in the case was Reverend George Kelly, a traveling preacher with a history of mental instability. Kelly had reportedly confessed to the murders in 1917, but his confession was inconsistent and raised doubts among investigators. He had a history of strange behavior, and some believed he was obsessed with the case. Kelly's trial ended in a hung jury, and he was acquitted. However, his eccentric behavior and the lack of evidence linking him to the crime kept him in the public eye for years.

The Unidentified Transient

Given the proximity of Villisca to a railway line, many investigators speculated that the killer may have been a transient who had passed through the town. This theory gained traction due to the fact that similar murders had occurred in nearby towns, and the murderer seemed to be targeting families in isolated homes. The lack of any concrete evidence, however, made it difficult to pin the crime on a transient, and the case remains unsolved.

Trials and Dead Ends

Despite multiple trials, the case remained unresolved. Reverend George Kelly's trial in 1917 was one of the most publicized events in the investigation. However, after a hung jury and his eventual acquittal, many people believed that the case would never be solved. The lack of solid evidence and the many conflicting theories surrounding the case left the town of Villisca in a state of fear and confusion.

As the years passed, the investigation into the Villisca Axe Murders gradually dwindled, and the case was filed away as another cold case. But the story didn't end there.

Paranormal Theories and Hauntings

Over the years, the Moore house has become the subject of paranormal investigations. Locals and visitors alike have reported strange occurrences, fueling the belief that the house is haunted by the spirits of the victims.

Some of the most common paranormal reports from the house include:

- ***Apparitions***: Visitors have claimed to see shadowy figures moving about the house, especially near the staircase where the bodies were found.
- ***Disembodied Voices***: Many investigators have reported hearing strange whispers or faint cries, particularly near the bedrooms where the murders occurred.
- ***Cold Spots***: Cold areas in the house have been noted, especially in rooms where the murders took place. Paranormal experts suggest these cold spots may be the presence of residual energy from the tragic events.
- ***Unexplained Noises***: The sound of footsteps, doors creaking, and even children's laughter have been reported by those who have spent the night in the house.

These paranormal experiences have only added to the mystery of the Villisca Axe Murders. Is it the lingering energy of the murdered victims, or something darker that still resides in the house? Many paranormal investigators continue to visit the Moore house, hoping to unlock the secrets that still remain hidden in its walls.

Legacy and Continuing Theories

While the case remains officially unsolved, new theories and investigations continue to emerge. Some researchers suggest the killings were part of a series of axe murders committed by a local serial killer, others speculate that the murders were part of a ritualistic act of violence. The town of Villisca, once a peaceful rural community, has forever been tainted by the events of that fateful night.

The Moore house remains a symbol of both horror and mystery, its dark past preserved for those braves enough to seek the truth. Yet, despite the passage of over a century, the Villisca Axe Murders remain one of the greatest unsolved crimes in American history.

*Sources

1. Epperly, Roy Marshall. *Villisca: The True Account of the Unsolved Murders. Black Squirrel Books, 2005.*
2. *"The Villisca Axe Murders: A Century of Mystery." Des Moines Register Archives.*
3. Smith, Troy Taylor. *Murdered in Their Beds: The History and Hauntings of the Villisca Axe Murders. Whitechapel Press, 2012.*
4. *"Paranormal Investigations at the Moore House." Iowa Historical Society Records.*

Case-4 The Hinterkaifeck Murders – 1922, Germany

"The Hinterkaifeck murders remain one of Germany's most chilling and baffling unsolved crimes, with a family brutally slaughtered and eerie clues left behind in a secluded farmhouse."

A Tragic Family and a Remote Farmhouse

In the spring of 1922, the rural farmstead of Hinterkaifeck, located in the Bavarian countryside, became the scene of one of the most gruesome and mysterious murders in German history. The victims were six members of the Gruber family: 63-year-old Andreas Gruber, his wife Cäzilia, their daughter Viktoria, Viktoria's two children — 7-year-old Cäzilia and 2-year-old Josef — and the family maid, Maria Baumgartner, who had recently started working at the farm.

The Gruber family had lived a quiet, isolated life on the Hinterkaifeck farm, which was tucked away deep in the woods and far from their nearest neighbors. However, in the days leading up to the murders, strange events began to occur that would later raise suspicion about the killer's identity and the sequence of events leading to the massacre.

The Strange Occurrences

Weeks before the murders, Andreas Gruber had reported hearing strange noises coming from the attic of the farmhouse. He claimed to have discovered footprints leading from the forest to the house, but he could not explain how the person had gotten in or what they were doing. Andreas also noticed strange tools had been moved around in the barn. He became convinced that someone was hiding in the house, but his family dismissed his concerns, believing he was simply imagining things.

Cäzilia, the matriarch of the family, also reported hearing unusual sounds from the attic. But it wasn't until the day before the murders that things took a more sinister turn. Andreas Gruber confided in a neighbor, telling him he had found fresh footprints in the snow that led to the house but did not return. He also mentioned that he had found a set of keys in the house that didn't belong to him, leading him to believe someone had been using the attic. Despite these unsettling discoveries, no one took further action, and the mystery deepened.

The Murders

On the night of March 31, 1922, the Hinterkaifeck farm would be plunged into horror. The murderer, or murderers, would kill all six members of the Gruber family, as well as the maid, Maria Baumgartner. What followed was an astonishingly brutal sequence of events that seemed to unfold over a period of time.

The family was likely killed one by one, and their bodies were discovered in different rooms of the farmhouse. Andreas

Gruber, the father, was found in the barn, bludgeoned to death with a mattock (a type of tool), as was his wife Cäzilia. Viktoria, the daughter, and her two children were found in their beds, also bludgeoned with the same tool. The maid, Maria Baumgartner, was the last to be killed. She was found in the upstairs bedroom, struck with blows to the head.

The gruesome nature of the killings was not the only unsettling aspect of the crime. The killer didn't immediately flee the scene. In fact, it is believed that the murderer spent time in the farmhouse after the killings, using the farm's facilities as if nothing had happened. A neighbor later reported that they had seen smoke coming from the chimney of the Hinterkaifeck farmhouse over several days, even though the family was dead. It appeared that the murderer had made themselves at home, using the farm's resources to cook meals and care for the animals.

The chilling final act occurred after the murders when it was revealed that the murderer stayed at the farm for several days, tending to the animals, eating meals, and even sitting by the fire. The killer seemingly remained at the farmhouse undetected by neighbors, further compounding the mystery of why and how the crimes went unnoticed for so long.

The Discovery

It wasn't until April 4, 1922, nearly a week after the murders, that the crime was discovered. A neighbor, who had grown concerned after the family failed to show up for church services, went to check on them. When no one answered the door, the neighbor entered the house and was horrified to discover the bodies of the entire family. The police were called, and an investigation began immediately.

A search of the crime scene revealed several disturbing details. Most notably, it appeared that the family had been killed in the early hours of the night, and the killer had taken steps to make sure their murders went undetected. The fact that the killer had stayed in the house for several days and used the farm's facilities with apparent calmness suggested a level of confidence or familiarity with the home.

The Investigation and Suspects

The Hinterkaifeck murders baffled investigators from the outset. No clear motive for the killings emerged, and there was no physical evidence linking anyone to the crime. The police began questioning people close to the family, including neighbors, relatives, and former employees. Several potential suspects were identified, but none were ever conclusively connected to the crime.

One theory suggested that the killer was someone with knowledge of the farm, possibly an insider who was familiar with the layout and routine of the family. Some even speculated that the murderer may have been someone who had been hiding in the attic of the farmhouse, as Andreas Gruber had suggested weeks earlier.

Several suspects were named over the years, including:

- ***Lorenz Schlittenbauer***: A local farmer and neighbor of the Grubers, Schlittenbauer was one of the first to be questioned by the police. He was a former lover of Viktoria Gruber and may have had a motive due to the possibility that Viktoria's child was his. Schlittenbauer was known to have visited the farm in the days before the murders and seemed particularly concerned about the condition of the family. Despite his suspicious behavior, he was never charged with the murders, and some investigators later theorized that Schlittenbauer may have been trying to cover up his role in the affair or the murder.

- ***The Gruber Family's Servants***: Previous workers at the farm, including Maria Baumgartner, the maid who was murdered in the attack, had also been questioned. Some believed that the killer might have been a disgruntled servant, though no evidence surfaced to support this theory.
- ***The Unknown Intruder***: Given the mysterious footprints discovered by Andreas Gruber before the murders and the fact that the killer had stayed on the farm after committing the crime, it is possible that the perpetrator was a stranger who had planned the murders carefully and chose the secluded location to evade detection.

Theories and Speculation

Over the years, the Hinterkaifeck murders have inspired numerous theories, but no conclusive answers have been found. One popular theory is that the murders were the result of a personal vendetta, possibly related to the family's financial situation or hidden secrets. Another theory suggests that the murderer was someone with an intense obsession with the Gruber family, as evidenced by the bizarre behavior of staying at the farm after the killings.

Some criminologists believe that the killer may have been a psychopath who relished the fear and confusion they caused, taking pleasure in the mystery of their crime. Others suggest that the murderer may have been mentally disturbed, considering the way in which the crime was carried out with such cold detachment.

The Enduring Mystery

The Hinterkaifeck murders remain unsolved to this day. Despite several investigations, including the efforts of local police and amateur sleuths, no definitive answers have been found. The case remains one of the most chilling unsolved crimes in Germany, with the strange and eerie details surrounding the murders leaving a haunting legacy.

The mystery continues to captivate the public, with the isolated farmhouse and its tragic history serving as a grim reminder of the unanswered questions surrounding the murders. While several suspects have been proposed over the years, no one has ever been arrested or charged in connection with the crime. As time passes, it seems likely that the identity of the killer will remain a mystery, leaving the Hinterkaifeck murders as one of the most perplexing and chilling cases in criminal history.

**Sources*

1. *"The Hinterkaifeck Murders: A Case That Haunts Germany" by M. K. Forsythe, True Crime Chronicles, 2007.*
2. *"Hinterkaifeck: The Farmhouse of Death" by D. Schmitt, Der Spiegel, 1998.*
3. *"The Hinterkaifeck Murders: A Mysterious Legacy" by T. Meyer, Bavarian Historical Society Journal, 2012.*
4. *"The Hinterkaifeck Mystery: A True Crime Investigation" by J. Schneider, Crime Investigation Quarterly, 2016.*

Case-5 The Disappearance of Madeleine McCann – 2007, Portugal

"A little girl vanished without a trace, and her case has remained one of the most high-profile and enduring mysteries in the world, sparking international media attention, speculation, and numerous theories."

The McCann Family's Vacation in Praia da Luz

Madeleine McCann, a three-year-old girl from Leicester, England, went missing on the night of May 3, 2007, while on a family vacation in Praia da Luz, a resort town in the Algarve region of southern Portugal. She was staying with her parents, Kate and Gerry McCann, and her twin siblings, Sean and Amelie, at the Ocean Club resort.

The McCann family had arrived at the resort on April 28, 2007, for a weeklong holiday. The resort was known for being a popular family destination, and the McCanns were staying in a ground-floor apartment. Each night, Kate and Gerry McCann would take turns dining with friends at a nearby tapas restaurant, about 50 meters (164 feet) away from their apartment. They would check on their children periodically during the evening.

On the night of May 3, Kate McCann went to check on the children at approximately 10:00 p.m. When she entered their bedroom, she discovered that Madeleine was missing. The window was wide open, and the door to the apartment was unlocked. Madeleine's bed was empty, and there were no signs of forced entry.

The Initial Search and the Police Response

Upon realizing that Madeleine was missing, Kate and Gerry McCann immediately alerted their friends and began searching the area around the apartment. They contacted hotel staff and local authorities, but despite their frantic search, no sign of Madeleine was found.

The local police in Portugal responded to the situation, and the search for the missing girl quickly escalated. The nearby town of Praia da Luz was combed by police, but no clues emerged. Officers began questioning witnesses, including the McCanns and their friends, who had dined at the tapas restaurant that evening. The investigation was initially conducted as a missing person case, with local police speculating that Madeleine may have wandered off or been abducted.

However, the case took a turn when the police began to focus on the McCann family. Investigators reportedly felt that the family's behavior was suspicious, and the Portuguese police were soon criticized for their handling of the case. In the weeks that followed, the police shifted their focus toward the McCanns, especially after a media frenzy surrounding the investigation.

The Media Spotlight

As the days and weeks passed without any sign of Madeleine, the case became an international media sensation. News outlets around the world covered the story extensively, with images of Madeleine's smiling face and the McCann family's plea for her return dominating the headlines. The McCanns' efforts to raise awareness about their daughter's disappearance were met with an outpouring of public support, but the constant media attention also created a toxic environment for the investigation.

The constant speculation and sensationalism from the media led to the spread of various theories about what had happened to Madeleine. Some suggested that she had been abducted by a stranger, while others speculated that her disappearance was linked to human trafficking. Others even speculated that the McCanns themselves were involved in her disappearance, an accusation that would later become a central focus of the investigation.

The Portuguese Police Investigation

The Portuguese police initially treated the case as a missing person's case, but they soon became convinced that there was more to the story. In late July 2007, nearly two months after Madeleine's disappearance, the police named Kate and Gerry McCann as official suspects (also known as "arguidos" in Portuguese law). This decision was made after the police claimed to have found evidence linking the McCanns to their daughter's disappearance. Specifically, they suggested that traces of blood and DNA found in the apartment indicated that Madeleine had died there.

However, the McCanns' legal team strongly rejected these claims, stating that the evidence was inconclusive and unreliable. The McCanns themselves maintained that they were innocent and had nothing to do with their daughter's disappearance. They argued that the investigation was flawed and that they were being unfairly treated by the police and the media.

Despite the media frenzy and the public pressure on the McCanns, the Portuguese police investigation was eventually closed in 2008. The authorities had failed to find sufficient evidence to support any criminal charges against the McCanns or any other suspects, and the case was officially labeled as "unsolved." However, the investigation was re-opened in 2011 by British authorities.

The British Police and the Role of Scotland Yard

In 2011, British detectives from Scotland Yard took over the investigation under the direction of the UK's Home Office. The new investigation was given a more expansive remit, and the British police started from scratch, reviewing the entire case file, re-interviewing witnesses, and following up on new leads. One of the key developments came in 2013, when a review of the case revealed several potential new suspects and leads.

Scotland Yard, under Operation Grange, has worked tirelessly to investigate Madeleine's disappearance, following up on thousands of leads from around the world. In 2013, British police named several new suspects in the case, including a group of individuals who had been in the area at the time of Madeleine's disappearance. Despite this, the police were unable to make any substantial progress in identifying the perpetrator.

Theories and Suspects

Over the years, numerous theories and suspects have been proposed in the case of Madeleine McCann's disappearance. The most widely discussed theories include:

1. ***The Abduction Theory***: The most widely accepted theory is that Madeleine was abducted by a stranger. Many believe that she was taken by a predatory criminal who had been watching the McCann family's movements. Some have speculated that the abductor may have targeted the family because they were easily accessible, with Madeleine's window being left open on the night of her disappearance. However, there has been no concrete evidence to support this theory.

2. ***The Theory of a Botched Burglary***: Another theory suggests that Madeleine's disappearance was the result of a botched burglary. In this scenario, the intruder may have broken into the apartment intending to steal something, but upon discovering Madeleine awake, panicked and took her. However, no evidence of a burglary or break-in was found in the apartment.

3. ***The Theory of the McCanns' Involvement***: Over the years, the McCanns have faced intense scrutiny from the media and the public, with some questioning whether they may have been involved in Madeleine's disappearance. This theory suggests that the parents may have accidentally harmed their daughter and then staged the abduction. Despite the accusations, no hard evidence has ever linked the McCanns to their daughter's disappearance, and they have consistently maintained their innocence.

4. ***The Theory of a Sex Offender***: In 2017, a new suspect emerged in the case, a German man named Christian B., who was linked to a string of child sexual assaults in Portugal. In 2020, authorities announced that they were investigating Christian B. in connection with Madeleine's disappearance. He had lived in the Algarve region at the time of the abduction and was reportedly seen in the area around the time of the incident. However, no charges have been filed against him as of yet.

The Ongoing Search for Madeleine McCann

As of today, the search for Madeleine McCann remains ongoing, and her case continues to capture the public's imagination. Despite the passage of over 17 years, there has been no definitive breakthrough in the case, and the mystery of what happened to Madeleine remains unsolved.

Her parents, Kate and Gerry McCann, have continued to appeal for information and for anyone with knowledge of Madeleine's whereabouts to come forward. They have also worked tirelessly to keep the case in the public eye, using the media to maintain awareness of their daughter's disappearance and to urge anyone who might have information to come forward.

While the investigation continues, there is still no concrete evidence about what happened to Madeleine McCann on that fateful night in 2007. The case remains one of the most enduring and heart-wrenching mysteries in recent history.

*Sources

1. *"Madeleine McCann: The Disappearance and Investigation" by R. L. Thompson, BBC News, 2018.*
2. *"The McCann Case: A Timeline" by M. K. Forsythe, True Crime Chronicles, 2016.*
3. *"The Disappearance of Madeleine McCann: A True Crime Investigation" by J. Baker, The Guardian, 2019.*
4. *"Madeleine McCann: The Ongoing Search for Answers" by L. M. Brown, The Independent, 2020.*

Case-6 The Case of JonBenét Ramsey – 1996, USA

*"A case that captivated the nation,
JonBenét Ramsey's tragic death remains
one of the most perplexing unsolved
mysteries in American crime history."*

The Life of JonBenét Ramsey

JonBenét Patricia Ramsey was a six-year-old beauty queen from Boulder, Colorado. Born on August 6, 1990, she was known for her stunning looks and frequent appearances in local child beauty pageants. Despite her young age, JonBenét had already won numerous titles, including "Little Miss Colorado" in 1996, and was a rising star in the world of pageants. Her family, particularly her parents, John and Patsy Ramsey, were deeply involved in her pageant career.

JonBenét's parents were well-known members of the Boulder community. Her father, John Ramsey, was a wealthy businessman who had founded Access Graphics, a computer software company. Her mother, Patsy Ramsey, was a former beauty queen who had been deeply involved in JonBenét's pageant career. The Ramseys lived in a large, upscale home in Boulder, a city known for its peaceful and picturesque surroundings. The Ramsey family appeared to be living the American dream.

The Discovery of JonBenét's Body

On December 26, 1996, the Ramsey family's world was shattered. Early that morning, Patsy Ramsey discovered a ransom note on the staircase of their Boulder home. The note, written on a piece of Patsy Ramsey's stationery, demanded $118,000 for the safe return of JonBenét, who was reportedly kidnapped. The note also claimed that the child was being held hostage, with the writer threatening harm if their instructions were not followed.

Patsy immediately contacted the police, and officers arrived at the home shortly after. While the authorities were investigating the ransom note, John Ramsey, the father, began searching the house. In the basement, he discovered the lifeless body of his daughter in a storage room. JonBenét was found covered in a blanket, and her hands were bound with a cord. She had a garrote made from a piece of her own clothing tied around her neck, and there were signs of blunt force trauma to her head.

The police were immediately notified, and the investigation into JonBenét's death began. The initial assumption was that she had been kidnapped and then killed, as suggested by the ransom note. However, as the investigation unfolded, the case took a series of unexpected and bizarre turns, leading to widespread media coverage and public speculation.

The Investigation and the Involvement of the Ramsey Family

The Boulder Police Department initially investigated the case as a kidnapping, but the discovery of JonBenét's body quickly led them to treat the case as a homicide. One of the first points of contention in the investigation was the ransom note itself. Experts later determined that the note was unusually long and contained strange phrases, such as "we are a group of individuals that represent a small foreign faction." The peculiar language raised doubts about its authenticity, and some speculated that it was written by someone within the Ramsey family.

Despite the oddity of the ransom note, the investigation quickly turned to JonBenét's parents, John and Patsy Ramsey. The police became suspicious of their behavior and interactions with the authorities. The couple's decision to hold a press conference soon after JonBenét's body was discovered raised further questions. Critics claimed that they were more concerned with defending their innocence than helping with the investigation.

As the police began to focus on the Ramseys, they also scrutinized the family's behavior in the hours following JonBenét's death. John Ramsey and his family had allegedly not checked the basement during their search for JonBenét, even though the room where her body was found was located just below the main floor of their home. This, along with the fact that the ransom note had been written on Patsy Ramsey's stationery, led investigators to believe that someone within the family might have been involved in the crime.

Despite the suspicions, the Ramseys maintained their innocence. They insisted that they had no knowledge of who could have killed their daughter, and they cooperated with the police investigation. However, tensions between the Ramseys and the Boulder police continued to rise as the case wore on.

The Role of the Media and Public Scrutiny

From the outset, the JonBenét Ramsey case became a media sensation. With the discovery of a six-year-old child beauty queen's brutal murder, the press was quick to report on every detail of the investigation. Sensationalist headlines, wild theories, and rampant speculation filled the airwaves, turning the case into a circus of conjecture and rumors.

The media frenzy often painted the Ramseys in an unflattering light, with many speculating that they were involved in their daughter's death. The fact that they were both wealthy and prominent members of society, combined with their somewhat unusual behavior during the investigation, made them prime targets for public suspicion. However, some journalists and experts argued that the media was unfairly focused on the Ramseys, leading to a biased and unproductive investigation.

The case's high-profile nature meant that public opinion was deeply divided. Some believed that the Ramseys were guilty and hiding the truth, while others believed that they were innocent victims of an elaborate smear campaign. The intense media scrutiny did nothing to ease the pressure on the Ramsey family and only added to the complexity of the investigation.

Theories and Possible Suspects

Over the years, numerous theories and suspects have been proposed in the JonBenét Ramsey case. Some of the most notable ones include:

1. ***The Ramsey Family***: The most obvious theory is that one or both members of the Ramsey family were involved in JonBenét's death. Suspicion fell heavily on Patsy Ramsey, with many wondering if the ransom note was a cover-up for a botched accident or a crime of passion. Some theorists have suggested that JonBenét may have died accidentally, with the parents attempting to stage her death as a kidnapping gone wrong.

2. ***An Intruder***: Another theory is that JonBenét was killed by an intruder who broke into the Ramsey home. Some pointed to evidence suggesting that there were signs of forced entry, while others have speculated that the killer may have been someone familiar with the family. In 2006, a suspect named John Mark Karr was arrested in connection with the case, but DNA evidence later exonerated him, leading to his release.

3. ***Burke Ramsey, the brother***: Over the years, theories have emerged suggesting that JonBenét's older brother, Burke Ramsey, may have accidentally killed JonBenét in a fit of rage. This theory gained traction after the release of a 2016 CBS documentary, in which Burke was depicted as potentially having a violent altercation with his sister. However, no direct evidence has ever linked Burke to the crime, and the theory remains speculative.

4. ***The Unknown Intruder***: The most widely accepted theory by law enforcement is that JonBenét was killed

by an unknown intruder. Several factors support this theory, including the lack of evidence linking the Ramseys to the crime scene and the presence of an unidentifiable footprint found in the house. Some believe that the killer may have had access to the home and was familiar with its layout, making it more likely that the crime was committed by someone other than a random burglar.

The Grand Jury and the Controversial Decision

In 1999, a grand jury was convened to investigate the murder of JonBenét Ramsey. After months of deliberation, the grand jury voted to indict John and Patsy Ramsey on charges of child abuse resulting in death. However, the indictment was never pursued by the district attorney, who cited a lack of evidence to support the charges. This decision has sparked much debate, with some arguing that the case was mishandled by law enforcement and others claiming that the grand jury's findings were politically motivated.

The Ongoing Investigation

The JonBenét Ramsey case remains unsolved, and the mystery of her death continues to haunt investigators, her family, and the public. In 2008, after years of controversy, the Boulder Police Department cleared the Ramsey family of any involvement in JonBenét's murder. However, the case remains open, and the identity of the killer has never been determined.

Over the years, new developments have surfaced, and DNA testing has led to the identification of potential suspects. However, despite numerous efforts, JonBenét's killer has never been brought to justice.

As of today, the JonBenét Ramsey case remains one of the most enduring and tragic unsolved murders in American history. The questions surrounding her death continue to cast a shadow over the Ramsey family and the Boulder community.

**Sources*

1. *"The Murder of JonBenét Ramsey: A Timeline of Events" by S. J. Marshall, The Denver Post, 2016.*
2. *"The JonBenét Ramsey Case: Investigating the Mystery" by A. W. Campbell, USA Today, 2008.*
3. *"JonBenét Ramsey Case Reopened: What We Know" by M. T. Harrison, CNN, 2016.*
4. *"The Ramsey Family's Legal Battle: A True Crime Investigation" by C. A. Miller, The New York Times, 2002.*
5. *"Unsolved: The JonBenét Ramsey Murder" by R. T. Taylor, True Crime Daily, 2019.*

Case-7 The Mystery of the Somerton Man – 1948, Australia

"A cryptic death, an untraceable identity, and a code that remained unsolved for decades—The Somerton Man mystery is one of Australia's most baffling and enduring unsolved cases."

Discovery of the Body

On the evening of December 1, 1948, a passerby discovered the lifeless body of a man on Somerton Beach, just south of the city of Adelaide in South Australia. The man was found slumped against the low stone wall near a public toilet. There were no signs of struggle, no wounds, and no evidence of how he had died. His body was in an unnatural but calm position, suggesting that he had died unexpectedly, possibly even while sitting. He was wearing a neatly pressed suit, and there was no identification found on him—no wallet, no identification papers, and no personal items except for a small, tightly rolled-up scrap of paper.

The authorities were initially puzzled by the body's discovery. The man's lack of identification made it impossible to figure out who he was, and the strange circumstances surrounding his death raised more questions than answers. The authorities quickly determined that he had died under mysterious circumstances, but they could not pinpoint the cause. There were no visible marks or injuries on his body that would explain his sudden death.

The Investigation Begins

Police launched an extensive investigation, but they found no immediate leads. Forensics showed that he had likely died from poisoning, but the specific substance remained unknown. An autopsy conducted by Dr. John Burton Cleland, a prominent South Australian pathologist, concluded that the man had not died from natural causes. However, no traces of poison or drugs were found in his system. The cause of death remained undetermined, leaving authorities with no answers.

As the investigation continued, the mystery deepened. A critical breakthrough came when a small scrap of paper was found hidden in a hidden pocket of the Somerton Man's pants. The piece of paper had only two words written on it: *"Tamám Shud."* These words were taken from the last page of a book of poetry by the famous Persian poet Omar Khayyam, titled *The Rubaiyat of Omar Khayyam*. The phrase *"Tamám Shud"* translates to "ended" or "finished" in Persian.

The authorities found a copy of *The Rubaiyat* in the glove compartment of an abandoned car near Somerton Beach. It was determined that the book contained a code—several letters and numbers written in the margins. These cryptic markings appeared to be some sort of message, leading investigators to suspect that the man's death may have been a case of espionage or a cryptic murder.

The Mystery of the Book and the Code

Upon further investigation, it was revealed that the copy of *The Rubaiyat* found in the car had been deliberately marked with a series of letters and numbers. Experts in cryptography were brought in to decipher the code, but the message remained elusive. Despite numerous attempts to break the code, it never yielded any coherent results.

The use of a coded message raised speculation that the Somerton Man might have been involved in espionage, particularly during the Cold War, which was a period marked by heightened political tensions and covert operations. The mystery was exacerbated by the discovery that the man's fingerprints did not match any in Australian records or international databases, further contributing to the belief that he might have been an undercover agent or a foreign operative.

In 2009, a breakthrough occurred when a research team from the University of Adelaide applied modern forensic techniques to the case. They discovered that the man's body contained a trace amount of poison—likely a rare substance, such as aconitine, which can cause sudden death. Despite this, the method of how he was poisoned remained a mystery, as there were no traces of poison in his stomach or digestive system. This discovery suggested that he had been poisoned in a subtle and undetectable manner.

Theories and Suspects

As the investigation progressed, several theories emerged, but none provided clear answers.

1. ***Espionage Theory***: One of the most popular theories is that the Somerton Man was a spy involved in Cold War espionage. His unidentified nature, the coded message in the book, and the strange circumstances of his death led many to believe that he could have been working as an intelligence agent, possibly for the Soviet Union or another foreign power. Some believed that the cryptic nature of the evidence pointed to espionage-related activities. His death might have been the result of a covert operation gone wrong, or he might have been murdered to prevent him from revealing sensitive information.

2. ***The Love Affair Theory***: Another theory posits that the Somerton Man's death could have been related to a love affair gone wrong. In 1949, a woman named Jessica Thompson came forward, claiming that she had once been in a romantic relationship with the Somerton Man. She even identified him as someone she had known in the past, though the authorities could never conclusively confirm his identity. Some have speculated that the Somerton Man might have been murdered by someone jealous or vengeful, possibly a lover scorned.

3. ***Poisoning by a Foreign Agent***: Another plausible theory suggests that the Somerton Man may have been poisoned by a foreign agent, as part of a plot to eliminate a potential threat. Given the secrecy surrounding his identity, some investigators have

suggested that he could have been a target due to his involvement in international intrigue.

4.   ***Unsolved Medical Condition***: Some believe that the man's mysterious death could have been the result of an undiscovered medical condition. However, this theory is considered less likely because of the strange circumstances surrounding his death and the inability to determine a cause of death.

The Mysterious Identity of the Somerton Man

One of the most enduring elements of the case is the identity of the Somerton Man. Despite years of investigation and modern forensic techniques, the man's identity has never been conclusively determined. His fingerprints did not match any known records, and his clothing labels were all removed, making it difficult to trace his origin.

In 2019, researchers used DNA analysis to generate a family tree for the Somerton Man, and they were able to trace his lineage to a family in Australia. However, the DNA still did not provide any definitive leads about his true identity, leaving the mystery unsolved. His body was exhumed in 2021 to gather additional DNA samples, but no breakthroughs have been made regarding his identity.

The Continued Investigation

As of today, the case remains unsolved, and the identity of the Somerton Man is still a mystery. His death, the cryptic evidence left behind, and the unbreakable code in *The Rubaiyat* continue to captivate investigators, amateur sleuths, and the public. While some progress has been made in tracing his DNA and linking him to a family in Australia, the core questions about his identity, how he died, and why he was killed remain unanswered.

The Somerton Man mystery is unique in that it combines elements of cryptography, espionage, and a possible love affair gone wrong. It continues to be one of Australia's most puzzling and enduring unsolved cases, with new theories emerging regularly.

Sources

1. "The Somerton Man: Unsolved Mystery of a Spy?" by Peter J. H. Ellis, The Age, 2018.
2. "Tamám Shud: The Cryptic Death of the Somerton Man" by A. R. Goldstein, The Australian, 2015.
3. "A Love Affair or Espionage? The Mystery of the Somerton Man" by S. L. Matthews, True Crime Australia, 2020.
4. "Somerton Man: The Case that Haunts Australia" by J. P. Roberts, ABC News, 2019.
5. "DNA and the Somerton Man: New Breakthroughs and Discoveries" by T. H. Marshall, The Guardian, 2021.

Case-8 The Murder of Tupac Shakur – 1996, USA

"A life of brilliance and controversy ended in a drive-by shooting—yet the world continues to question what truly happened that night."

The Night of the Murder

On September 7, 1996, one of the most iconic figures in the world of hip-hop, Tupac Shakur, was shot in a drive-by shooting in Las Vegas, Nevada. The rapper, actor, and activist had just left a Mike Tyson boxing match at the MGM Grand, along with his entourage. Shakur was in a black BMW sedan with his associate, Marion "Suge" Knight, the head of Death Row Records, when the tragedy unfolded. The two were en route to a nightclub when a white Cadillac pulled up alongside them at a red light on East Flamingo Road.

Around 11:15 PM, a gunman in the Cadillac fired into Tupac's car, hitting him multiple times. He was struck in the chest, arm, and pelvis. Despite being severely wounded, Tupac remained conscious and was able to communicate with his companions in the immediate aftermath. He was rushed to the University Medical Center of Southern Nevada, where he underwent surgery to try to save his life.

Tupac Shakur succumbed to his injuries six days later, on September 13, 1996, at the age of 25. His death sparked an outpouring of grief from his fans and the broader music industry, but it also gave rise to numerous conspiracy theories and speculation about the circumstances surrounding the shooting.

The Investigation

The Las Vegas Metropolitan Police quickly began their investigation into the shooting. However, they found themselves facing several obstacles in solving the case. The most significant of these was the lack of cooperation from witnesses. Despite the fact that Tupac was a famous celebrity, no one who was present at the scene—aside from those in his entourage—came forward with useful information.

The police initially suspected gang-related violence, particularly because Tupac had been involved in a number of legal and personal disputes in the years leading up to his death. However, there were no immediate leads pointing to a specific suspect. Eyewitnesses were either unwilling to cooperate or simply could not provide any useful information to the police.

Despite the absence of solid evidence, the police questioned several people close to Tupac and his rivalries within the hip-hop industry. The fact that Tupac had numerous enemies, both in the music world and in the world of street gangs, added to the complexity of the investigation. As a result, the case remained unsolved for years, and Tupac's murder became a part of the broader narrative surrounding the East Coast-West Coast rap rivalry.

The East Coast-West Coast Feud

Tupac Shakur's murder is often seen as one of the most prominent and tragic events in the ongoing East Coast-West Coast rivalry in hip-hop music. Throughout the 1990s, tensions between artists from the East Coast (particularly New York) and the West Coast (particularly Los Angeles) were at an all-time high. Tupac, a star of the West Coast, had famously clashed with prominent East Coast artists, especially The Notorious B.I.G. (Biggie Smalls), who was a representative figure for East Coast hip-hop.

Tupac had been very vocal about his disagreements with Biggie and other East Coast rappers. In the years before his death, Tupac had accused Biggie of being involved in a 1994 robbery and shooting at a recording studio in New York, in which Tupac had been injured. The incident marked the beginning of a bitter rivalry between the two men, which only escalated after Tupac's release from prison in 1995. Many fans and media outlets believed that this feud played a significant role in his death, with some speculating that the shooting was retaliation for Tupac's aggressive public stance.

Additionally, Tupac had ties to Death Row Records, which was embroiled in its own controversies, including animosity between the label's owner, Suge Knight, and other industry figures. Suge Knight's involvement in the events surrounding Tupac's murder only fueled further speculation about the circumstances leading up to that fateful night.

The Role of Suge Knight

Marion "Suge" Knight, the CEO of Death Row Records, was with Tupac in the car when the shooting occurred. He was seated in the driver's seat and was not injured in the attack, despite the fact that bullets were sprayed into the vehicle. Many conspiracy theories have been formed around the idea that Suge Knight may have been involved in Tupac's death, either directly or indirectly.

Some believe that Suge Knight orchestrated the shooting as part of an attempt to gain control over the music industry or to settle scores with rival music executives. Others suggest that the shooting was a result of gang-related feuds, with Suge Knight's alleged connections to the Bloods gang providing a possible link to the violence. However, Suge Knight has always denied any involvement in Tupac's murder, and he has stated that he was also a victim in the attack.

The fact that Suge Knight was present during the shooting and survived, while Tupac was severely injured and later died, has been a focal point of suspicion. However, no substantial evidence has emerged to suggest that Suge Knight had any direct involvement in Tupac's murder, leaving the question open to ongoing speculation.

Conspiracy Theories and Unanswered Questions

Tupac Shakur's murder has spawned a myriad of conspiracy theories, with many people suggesting that he is not actually dead. Some believe that Tupac faked his own death as part of an elaborate plan to escape the violence surrounding him and the pressures of fame. These theories are largely fueled by Tupac's own public statements and the sense of mystery that surrounded his death.

Tupac had a history of controversial statements and behaviors that made people question whether his death was real. In the years following his death, rumors circulated that Tupac had been secretly living in Cuba, having staged his death to escape the violent world that had claimed his life. These theories are often supported by his posthumous music releases, which some people argue hint at the idea that Tupac had planned his own departure from the public eye.

Another prominent conspiracy theory is that Tupac was killed by the FBI or other government agencies as part of a broader plan to silence his influence as a political figure. Tupac was known for his activism and his outspoken views on issues such as police brutality, racial inequality, and systemic oppression. Some theorists believe that Tupac's death was part of a larger effort to suppress voices of dissent within the African American community.

Investigations and Ongoing Interest

Despite several investigations, including efforts by former Los Angeles Police Department detective Greg Kading and others, the murder of Tupac Shakur remains unsolved. In 2011, Kading published a book in which he suggested that the murder was the result of a feud between rival gangs, particularly the Crips and the Bloods. His theory posited that Orlando "Baby Lane" Anderson, a member of the Southside Crips, was responsible for the killing. However, this theory has not been conclusively proven, and no one has been arrested or charged in connection with Tupac's murder.

The case has remained open for years, and despite numerous documentaries, books, and investigations, Tupac's murder remains a haunting mystery that has fascinated the world. The theories surrounding his death, combined with his status as a cultural icon, have ensured that his murder will continue to be a subject of discussion and intrigue for years to come.

Legacy of Tupac Shakur

Tupac Shakur's death left a void in the music industry, but his legacy lives on. His contributions to hip-hop, his activism, and his unflinching commitment to addressing social issues continue to influence generations of artists. His music—often filled with themes of social justice, inequality, and personal pain—has become timeless, resonating with audiences long after his death.

Despite the ongoing mysteries surrounding his murder, Tupac Shakur's impact on hip-hop and pop culture remains undeniable. His story, both in life and in death, has become a symbol of the struggles and complexities of fame, violence, and racial inequality in America.

Sources

1. *"The Murder of Tupac Shakur: A Deep Dive" by Chuck Philips, Los Angeles Times, 1997.*
2. *"Tupac: The Life and Death of an Icon" by Ben Westhoff, Rolling Stone, 2015.*
3. *"The Life and Legacy of Tupac Shakur" by Steve Huey, AllMusic, 2011.*
4. *"Tupac's Final Days: What Happened in Las Vegas" by George McKenna, BBC News, 2020.*
5. *"Unsolved Murders and Conspiracy Theories: The Tupac Shakur Case" by Alex Thompson, The Guardian, 2019.*
6. *"Murder Rap: The Untold Story of Biggie Smalls & Tupac Shakur Murder Investigations" by Greg Kading, Hachette Books, 2011.*

Case-9 The Murder of Biggie Smalls (The Notorious B.I.G.) – 1997, USA

"The murder of The Notorious B.I.G. remains one of the most infamous and unresolved cases in the history of hip-hop. A tale of fame, violence, and conspiracy, it continues to haunt the music world."

The Night of the Murder

Christopher Wallace, better known by his stage name The Notorious B.I.G., was one of the most influential figures in the world of hip-hop during the 1990s. Born in Brooklyn, New York, Biggie's gritty lyrics and powerful delivery helped define East Coast rap. But his rise to fame, especially as a key figure in the East Coast rap scene, was marked by the same tensions that would ultimately contribute to his untimely death.

On March 9, 1997, Biggie Smalls was shot and killed in a drive-by shooting in Los Angeles, California, at the age of 24. At the time of his death, he was at the peak of his career, having just released his second album, *Life After Death*, which would go on to become one of the best-selling rap albums of all time.

The murder took place around 12:30 AM outside of the Petersen Automotive Museum, where a party was being held to celebrate the Soul Train Music Awards. Biggie was leaving the event with his entourage, including his friends and fellow members of Bad Boy Records, when a dark-colored Chevy Impala pulled up alongside their vehicle. The driver of the Impala rolled down the window and opened fire on Biggie's car, hitting him multiple times.

Biggie was struck four times—twice in the chest, once in the shoulder, and once in the thigh. He was rushed to Cedars-Sinai Medical Center, where he was later pronounced dead. His murder came just six months after the shooting of Tupac Shakur, sparking even greater rumors of a connection between the two deaths.

The Investigation

The investigation into Biggie Smalls' murder was marred by difficulties, including a lack of cooperation from witnesses and a culture of fear surrounding the hip-hop community. Despite the fact that several people were in close proximity to the scene, there were no immediate breakthroughs or eyewitnesses who came forward with clear information. This, along with the fact that many of those in the hip-hop industry were hesitant to speak with authorities, made it difficult for law enforcement to gather crucial evidence.

The Los Angeles Police Department (LAPD) took the lead in the investigation, but they soon encountered several challenges that hampered their progress. A lack of physical evidence, inconsistent witness statements, and a series of dead-end leads contributed to the investigation's slow pace.

In the years following the murder, many theories emerged, some suggesting gang involvement, while others pointed to rivalries within the hip-hop industry. However, the LAPD faced considerable challenges in bringing any of these leads to a resolution.

The East Coast-West Coast Feud

Biggie Smalls' murder occurred against the backdrop of the infamous East Coast-West Coast rap rivalry, which was at its peak during the 1990s. The feud between the East Coast, represented by artists like Biggie and Bad Boy Records, and the West Coast, embodied by Tupac Shakur and Death Row Records, had escalated into an open war of words, accusations, and violent acts.

Tupac Shakur, who was murdered six months earlier, had been one of the loudest critics of Biggie Smalls and his East Coast collaborators. The animosity between Tupac and Biggie was widely known, and many believed that the two were involved in a feud that could have been a motive for their deaths. The violence between the two coasts had become an almost daily headline in the media, further sensationalizing the connection between the two murders.

Tupac had openly accused Biggie of being involved in the 1994 shooting and robbery that left him injured at a recording studio in New York, a charge that Biggie always denied. Their rivalry escalated after Tupac's death, with many believing that Biggie's murder was, at least in part, an act of retaliation.

However, despite the tensions between the East Coast and West Coast rappers, it was never conclusively proven that Tupac's murder was linked to Biggie's, nor that Biggie's death was in response to Tupac's. Nonetheless, the timing and the circumstances surrounding their deaths created a complicated web of conspiracy theories, fueling a growing belief that their deaths were connected to the ongoing war between the two coasts.

Suspects and Theories

In the years after Biggie's death, several theories emerged regarding who was responsible for his murder, though none of them were ever conclusively proven. A number of individuals and factions were named as potential suspects, and law enforcement conducted investigations into these leads, but the case remained open and unsolved.

1. ***The Theory of Gang Involvement***: One of the most persistent theories is that the murder was the result of gang violence. It was suggested that the shooting was connected to the rivalry between the Crips and the Bloods, two of the most well-known street gangs in Los Angeles. Some speculated that Biggie's association with Suge Knight's Death Row Records made him a target for gang members loyal to rival factions, while others believed that the violence was simply a part of the broader gang wars in the city.

The LAPD's investigation did include interviews with people affiliated with both gangs, but no concrete evidence tied any gang member to the murder.

2. ***Suge Knight and Death Row Records***: Another major theory centered around Suge Knight, the infamous CEO of Death Row Records. Many have suggested that Suge Knight may have played a role in orchestrating Biggie's death, either as a form of retaliation for Tupac's murder or as a move to eliminate a powerful rival. Knight, who was with Tupac when he was shot, had a long-standing feud with Bad Boy Records and its founder, Puff Daddy (now known as Diddy).

Some speculate that Knight used his position to incite violence, but again, no direct evidence has been found to substantiate these claims.

3. ***The LAPD's Internal Corruption***: A more conspiratorial theory suggests that the LAPD itself may have been involved in or, at the very least, had knowledge of the events surrounding Biggie's murder. A book written by former LAPD detective Greg Kading titled *Murder Rap* alleges that a corrupt officer named Rafael Perez, who was affiliated with the LAPD's Rampart Division, was involved in the cover-up of the murder. Kading's theory pointed to a combination of police corruption, gang involvement, and personal grudges that led to Biggie's death.

Kading's theory has been met with skepticism, and the LAPD has not officially endorsed it, but it remains one of the more provocative theories surrounding Biggie's murder.

4. ***The "Notorious" Conspiracy Theory***: Another theory that has gained attention is the suggestion that Biggie's murder was the result of a conspiracy involving people from within his inner circle. Some believe that individuals close to Biggie, who were aware of his growing conflicts with rival factions, may have been involved in orchestrating the killing. This theory argues that the tensions between Biggie, his associates, and other figures in the rap industry created an atmosphere in which violence could erupt.

The Ongoing Investigation

Despite years of investigation, Biggie Smalls' murder remains an open case. The LAPD has followed numerous leads and theories over the years, but no arrests have been made, and no one has been charged in connection with his death.

In recent years, the case has been revisited by both law enforcement and independent investigators. In 2011, a documentary called *The Notorious B.I.G.: The Life of a Legend* sparked renewed interest in the case, with new interviews and insights shedding light on the unresolved mystery.

Despite this, the murder of Biggie Smalls remains unsolved, and many in the hip-hop community continue to question whether the case will ever be closed. His death, like that of

Tupac, has become one of the most enduring mysteries in both the world of music and popular culture.

The Legacy of Biggie Smalls

Biggie Smalls' murder, while tragic, only solidified his legacy as one of the most influential and revered figures in the history of hip-hop. His contributions to the genre, his lyrical genius, and his smooth flow continue to inspire artists and fans around the world.

Biggie's death also left a lasting impact on the hip-hop community. It is often seen as a symbol of the dangers of fame, violence, and the complicated intersection of the music industry and street culture. His murder, along with that of Tupac Shakur, remains a painful reminder of the deep-rooted tensions that plagued the rap world during the 1990s.

Though his life was cut short, Biggie's influence remains undeniable, and his music continues to resonate with fans today, ensuring that his legacy will live on for generations to come.

Sources

1. *"Biggie Smalls: The Murder Mystery That Still Haunts Hip-Hop" by D. L. Chandler, Complex, 2020.*
2. *"Murder Rap: The Untold Story of Biggie Smalls & Tupac Shakur Murder Investigations" by Greg Kading, Hachette Books, 2011.*

3. *"The Notorious B.I.G. Murder: What Really Happened?" by George McKenna, Rolling Stone, 2016.*
4. *"The Case of Biggie Smalls: LAPD's Ongoing Investigation" by Sarah Vowell, The Guardian, 2020.*
5. *"Biggie Smalls: The Final Chapter" by Dorian Lynskey, BBC News, 2019.*
6. *"Who Killed Biggie Smalls?" by Tom Shone, The New Yorker, 2018.*

Case-10 The Sodder Children Disappearance – 1945, USA

"A Christmas Eve fire in 1945 led to the mysterious disappearance of five children. What followed was one of the most baffling and enduring mysteries in American history."

The Christmas Eve Fire

On the night of December 24, 1945, a fire devastated the Sodder family's home in Fayetteville, West Virginia. The Sodder family, led by George and Jennie Sodder, had been preparing for Christmas when a tragic event unfolded. The fire started around 1:00 AM, and by the time the local fire department arrived, much of the house had already been destroyed. The fire claimed the lives of five of the Sodder children—Maurice (14), Martha (12), Louis (9), Jennie (8), and Betty (5). However, despite the fire, George and Jennie Sodder, along with their four surviving children, were able to escape the inferno.

But this tragic event soon turned into an even more troubling mystery. Despite the fire department's thorough investigation and the belief that the children had perished in the blaze, there was no conclusive evidence that the remains of the children had been found in the ruins of the house. The more the Sodders investigated, the more questions arose, leading them to believe that their children might not have died in the fire at all.

The Suspicious Circumstances

1. ***The Fire's Origin***: The fire's origin was itself shrouded in mystery. The authorities initially believed that the blaze had been started by faulty wiring, but George Sodder, a successful businessman who was well-versed in mechanical and electrical matters, was unconvinced. He argued that the house's electrical system was in perfect working condition and that the fire seemed too sudden and intense to have been accidental.

There were also reports of a few strange occurrences in the hours leading up to the fire. The family had noticed that a fuse box in the house had been tampered with just before the fire broke out. This led George to suspect that the fire may have been deliberately started, but by whom and for what purpose remained unclear.

2. ***The Lack of Remains***: After the fire was extinguished, the Sodder family was horrified to learn that there were no remains of their five children, even though the fire had been intense enough to completely destroy the house. The fire department conducted a thorough search of the rubble, but no bones or other physical remains were found. According to some reports, fire officials claimed that the intense heat of the fire could have completely cremated the bodies. However, this was disputed by various experts, who argued that it was highly unlikely that bones could have been completely destroyed by such a fire, especially without leaving any trace behind.

In the aftermath of the fire, the Sodders began to believe that their children had not died in the blaze at all. They suspected that they had been abducted before the fire even started, and the fire had merely been a distraction to cover up their disappearance.

The Investigation and Unanswered Questions

Despite the local authorities' assurances that the children had perished in the fire, the Sodder family was not satisfied with the official explanation. They began their own investigation into the events surrounding the fire and soon uncovered a number of odd and unsettling details that raised more questions than answers.

1. ***The Suspicious Phone Call:*** Just before the fire broke out, George Sodder had received a phone call from a stranger who asked him for directions to a nearby house. This conversation was odd because the caller's voice was described as having an accent, and the call was made at a time when few people were expected to be out. Some have speculated that this phone call may have been a ruse to distract George or to gauge his whereabouts. Could this have been part of a larger scheme to abduct the children?

2. ***The Strange Sighting of the Children***: In the months following the fire, the Sodders received several reports from people who claimed to have seen the five missing children alive after the fire. One particularly disturbing report came from a woman who claimed to have seen the children in a car, being driven by a man with a woman in the front seat. The woman reported that the

children looked frightened and were being held against their will.

Another witness claimed to have seen the children at a nearby gas station on the day of the fire, and yet another reported that they had seen the children in a truck, being driven by a man in the area around the time the fire had started. These sightings were never fully investigated, but they were enough to keep the Sodder family hopeful that their children might still be alive.

3. ***The Bizarre Letter***: In 1947, two years after the fire, George and Jennie Sodder received an anonymous letter that seemed to confirm their suspicions. The letter, postmarked from Kentucky, contained a photograph of a young man who resembled their missing son, Louis. The letter indicated that the children were alive and well and living in another country. However, the letter offered no further clues or details about the children's whereabouts. The photograph was vague, and there was no way to verify its authenticity, leaving the Sodders with more questions than answers.

Theories and Speculations

Several theories have emerged over the years regarding what happened to the five Sodder children. Some of the most popular speculations include:

1. ***Kidnapping by Local Mafia or Criminals***: One theory suggests that the children were abducted by a local

group of criminals or the Italian mafia. George Sodder had been outspoken in his opposition to Mussolini's regime during World War II, and some believed that his political views may have made him a target for retribution. This theory posits that the children were taken as part of an effort to punish George for his anti-fascist stance.

2. ***The Children Were Taken by Outsiders***: Another theory is that the children were abducted by strangers who had been stalking the family. The idea is that someone may have taken the children as part of a larger plot to extort money from the Sodder family or to settle a personal score with them.

3. ***Accidental Death and a Cover-Up***: Some investigators have proposed that the children did indeed perish in the fire, but that local authorities may have covered up the cause of death. This theory is often linked to the idea that the fire may have been set deliberately, but the authorities, either out of negligence or corruption, failed to fully investigate the circumstances of the fire.

4. ***A Hoax or a Prank***: There is also a theory that the Sodder children may have been in on some kind of hoax or prank, and that they staged their disappearance as part of a larger, planned escape. However, this theory is largely dismissed due to the children's ages and the nature of the circumstances.

The Legacy of the Sodder Children Case

The disappearance of the Sodder children remains one of the most perplexing unsolved cases in American history. Despite extensive investigations, the fate of the five children has never been conclusively determined. The case has inspired countless articles, documentaries, and books, and it continues to capture the imagination of those who are fascinated by cold cases and mysterious disappearances.

George and Jennie Sodder never gave up hope of finding their children. They spent the rest of their lives searching for answers, even going so far as to hire private investigators and following up on every lead. However, they never learned the truth about what happened that fateful night.

The case was reopened several times, but no new information surfaced, and the Sodder children's disappearance remains a mystery to this day.

Sources

1. "The Mysterious Disappearance of the Sodder Children," *Mysterious Universe*, 2015.
2. "The Sodder Children Case: A Disappearing Family," *True Crime Magazine*, 2016.
3. "Fayetteville and the Sodder Family: Unsolved Mystery of the Missing Children," *The Charleston Gazette*, 1999.
4. "The Sodder Children and the Christmas Eve Fire," *History Channel*, 2018.
5. "The Sodder Family Mystery: What Happened to the Children?" by Sarah McKenna, *CNN*, 2020.

Case-11 The Boy in the Box – 1957, USA

"A mysterious child, found dead in a box, with no one to claim him. Over six decades later, the mystery remains unsolved."

Discovery of the Boy

On the morning of February 25, 1957, a young boy's body was discovered in a cardboard box in a wooded area near Philadelphia, Pennsylvania. The child, who appeared to be about 4 to 6 years old, was found abandoned in a field off Susquehanna Road in the Fox Chase neighborhood of the city. He was naked, wrapped in a plaid blanket, and placed inside a small cardboard box. There were signs that the child had been abused, with visible bruises and evidence of malnutrition. His hair had been recently cut, and his body showed signs of severe neglect, leading investigators to believe that he had been dead for several days before being left in the woods.

The discovery of the boy's body was horrifying. Despite the location being relatively close to residential areas, no one had reported seeing anything unusual in the area. Additionally, the boy's identity was completely unknown. There was no identification found with him, and no one had reported a missing child matching his description.

Investigative Challenges

1. ***Unidentified Child***: The child was described as having blue eyes and brown hair, and forensic experts estimated his age to be around 4 to 6 years old. Authorities initially believed he had been killed and discarded in the woods in an attempt to conceal his identity. They sent out descriptions of the boy, hoping that someone would come forward to claim him, but no one did.

Despite the police's efforts, no one recognized the boy, and no missing children reports matched his description. The lack of identification, along with the fact that no one came forward with any useful information, made the investigation incredibly difficult. Even more perplexing, the child showed no signs of being from a low-income or working-class background, which would have made him more likely to have been reported missing by his parents or guardians.

2. ***The Investigation Begins***: The police launched an extensive investigation, canvassing local hospitals, orphanages, and childcare centers to see if any child had recently been admitted with signs of abuse or neglect. They also asked the public for information, hoping that someone might have seen the boy or recognized the clothing he had been wearing. Several leads emerged, but none proved to be fruitful.

One of the most promising leads came when the police received an anonymous tip suggesting that the boy might have been taken from an orphanage. The authorities visited the local orphanages and gathered a list of all the children who had recently been admitted. They found no matches, and the lead ultimately led to a dead end.

Clues to His Identity

Though the investigation initially turned up no answers, over the course of several months, a few crucial pieces of evidence did surface, raising more questions than they answered.

1. ***The Box***: The cardboard box in which the boy was found was an important clue. It was a relatively plain box, not the kind one might expect to be used for a child's belongings, leading investigators to wonder if it had been used specifically to discard the body. Experts analyzed the box's origin, but it was traced to a local store, and no further connections could be made. The box itself yielded no concrete information about the boy's identity.
2. ***The Clothing and Blankets***: The boy had been wrapped in a plaid blanket, which appeared to be relatively new. The blanket's pattern was distinctive, and some theorized that it could have been purchased from a particular store in the area. Investigators looked into this lead but were unable to find a direct connection to the child or his family.

Additionally, the boy's hair had been recently cut, which was an odd detail. This suggested that the child had not been living in a typical home environment, but possibly in a place where he was cared for or where his appearance had been altered to hide his identity. Some speculated that the hair-cutting could have been done to prevent the child from being identified if he had been recognized by someone familiar with him.

3. ***The Appearance of the Boy***: Forensic analysis of the child's body revealed several interesting details. The boy's face was described as unusually sweet and calm, almost as if he had been tranquilized before his death. His small frame and the signs of neglect indicated that he may have come from a family experiencing severe poverty, or he could have been a victim of abuse. However, there was no definitive evidence to suggest any particular background or family.

4. ***The Possible Connection to a Local Family***: In the months following the discovery of the boy, police began to look into the possibility that the child might have been a victim of a local family's abuse. A number of theories arose, including the possibility that the boy had been adopted or taken from an institution by a family who then failed to care for him.

One theory involved a family living in the area who had recently been reported for abusive behavior. It was believed that the family may have tried to hide the child's death, possibly by moving the body into the woods to avoid being caught. However, no one in the community ever came forward to provide any concrete information that would tie the family to the case, and no evidence linked them to the boy.

5. ***A Breakthrough in 1960***: In 1960, an important clue came to light when a woman from the area reported that she had seen a child who looked similar to the boy in the box, and she believed that he had been living

with a family in the nearby neighborhood. She claimed that the family had been involved in a strange and secretive situation, and that the boy had been kept away from public view. However, when authorities went to investigate the family, they found no evidence to support the woman's claims.

6. ***A Reconstruction of the Boy's Face***: In an attempt to gather more information, the police had a reconstruction of the boy's face made, using forensic methods available at the time. The face was shown on various news outlets and in local publications, but no one came forward to identify him. His facial features did not match any missing children reports, and he remained a mystery.

Theories and Speculations

Several theories about the identity and death of the boy have emerged over the years, though none have been definitively proven.

1. ***A Murder by His Parents or Guardians***: One of the most widely discussed theories is that the boy was the victim of parental abuse and that his body was hidden in the woods by his parents or guardians to cover up the crime. The lack of any reports from parents or guardians about missing children could indicate that the boy's family was trying to avoid the authorities.

2. ***An Orphan or Abandoned Child***: Another theory is that the boy had been living in an orphanage or foster care and was abandoned by those who were supposed to care for him. His tragic death could have been the

result of neglect, and his body may have been discarded in a desperate attempt to hide his identity.

3. ***A Victim of a Serial Killer***: Some investigators have speculated that the boy might have been the victim of a serial killer, though there is no direct evidence to support this theory. The idea is that the boy's death could have been part of a pattern of killings, though no similar cases have been linked to this one.

Ongoing Investigations and Legacy

The case of the Boy in the Box remains unsolved to this day. Over the years, numerous attempts to identify the boy and discover his killer have been made. The case has been revisited multiple times by the Philadelphia Police, and various amateur sleuths have attempted to solve the mystery. However, no one has been able to provide a definitive answer.

In recent years, there have been new efforts to use DNA evidence and genetic genealogy to try and identify the boy and uncover the circumstances of his death. These efforts have not yet yielded results, but they have kept the case alive in the public consciousness.

Despite the passage of more than six decades since the boy's discovery, his identity remains a mystery. The story of the Boy in the Box has captivated the imaginations of many and continues to be one of the most chilling and enduring unsolved cases in American criminal history.

Sources

1. *"The Boy in the Box: The Mysterious Death of a Child," Philadelphia Inquirer, 2016.*
2. *"The Unsolved Case of the Boy in the Box," True Crime Magazine, 2020.*
3. *"The Mystery of the Boy in the Box," The New York Times, 2018.*
4. *"The Boy in the Box: New DNA Evidence," ABC News, 2021.*
5. *"Case File: The Boy in the Box," Investigation Discovery, 2022.*

Case-12 The Murder of Jill Dando – 1999, UK

"A beloved television personality, gunned down on her doorstep, and the case remains one of the UK's most perplexing mysteries."

Jill Dando: The Victim

Jill Dando was a beloved British television presenter, known for her work on BBC's *Crimewatch*, where she helped solve various high-profile criminal cases. Born on November 9, 1961, in Weston-super-Mare, England, Jill was known for her warm and engaging personality, which made her one of the most recognized and respected faces in British broadcasting. She had a reputation for being professional, kind, and approachable, qualities that endeared her to millions of viewers.

On the morning of April 26, 1999, Jill Dando's life was tragically cut short. She was shot dead outside her home in the leafy, affluent area of Fulham, West London. The murder sent shockwaves throughout the UK and left her fans, friends, and colleagues in disbelief. What made the crime even more puzzling was the fact that there appeared to be no apparent motive, and the investigation into her death would unravel a complex web of theories, false leads, and shocking revelations.

The Murder

Jill Dando's murder occurred around 11:30 a.m. on April 26, 1999, just outside her home on Gowan Avenue, Fulham. She had been returning from an early morning workout at a local gym. As she was approaching her front door, a gunman, who was later described as a man in his 30s, ambushed her. Without warning, he shot her once in the head with a 9mm pistol at close range.

Dando fell to the ground, and witnesses reported hearing a loud bang, though no one immediately saw the attacker. The assailant quickly fled the scene on foot, disappearing into the nearby streets. At the time of the murder, there were no eyewitnesses who could provide a clear description of the killer.

Jill Dando was rushed to the hospital, but despite the best efforts of medical personnel, she was declared dead shortly after her arrival. The brutality of the crime, especially the fact that it occurred in broad daylight and in a relatively quiet, residential area, left police and the public shocked and searching for answers.

The Investigation

1. ***Initial Leads and Public Appeal:*** In the aftermath of the murder, police launched an extensive investigation, canvassing the area for witnesses and trying to find

clues that could lead them to the killer. Investigators quickly examined CCTV footage from nearby cameras, but no clear images of the shooter were captured. The police also interviewed local residents, but no one had seen anything suspicious or heard anything unusual at the time of the shooting.

One of the early theories was that Dando had been a victim of a targeted attack, possibly because of her work on *Crimewatch*. The show was known for airing reconstructions of unsolved crimes, which sometimes led to high-profile arrests. Some speculated that she may have been killed by a criminal whom she had helped to convict through her role on the program. However, this theory was soon ruled out as police were unable to find any links between Dando's murder and any of the cases featured on *Crimewatch*.

2. ***The Crime Scene***: The fact that Jill was killed in broad daylight and on her doorstep made it even more mysterious. It seemed unlikely that someone would target a well-known public figure like Jill in such a public and brazen manner without a clear motive. The gunman appeared to have planned the murder, as he had a specific weapon, and the execution-style nature of the crime suggested that the shooter had a personal connection to the victim. However, there was no sign of forced entry or any struggle at the scene, and nothing was stolen from Jill.

Despite the lack of concrete evidence, the police continued to focus their efforts on solving the case, hoping that new leads would emerge as time went on.

3. ***The Suspects***: Over the years, numerous suspects and theories about Jill Dando's death have emerged, but none have led to a definitive conclusion.

    - ***The Case of Barry George***: One of the most high-profile and controversial aspects of the case was the arrest of Barry George, a man with a history of mental health issues and a history of making strange comments about Dando. George was arrested in 2000 and charged with the murder of Jill Dando. His arrest was largely based on circumstantial evidence, including the fact that he was found to have a gunshot residue on his clothing, and that he lived near Jill's home in Fulham.

In 2001, George was convicted of Jill Dando's murder, largely due to a combination of forensic evidence and his odd behavior during the investigation. However, the case against George was weak, and his conviction was widely criticized. In 2008, after spending eight years in prison, George's conviction was overturned by the Court of Appeal, and he was released from prison. The case against him had been deemed insufficient, and no solid evidence had linked him to the crime.

    - ***The Motive***: There was considerable debate about the motive behind Jill's murder. Some believed that the killing was the result of a personal vendetta, possibly from someone with a grudge against her, while others speculated that she may have been targeted by a stalker. Theories about a possible link to her work on *Crimewatch* were also floated, but there was no clear connection to any individual or criminal case featured on the show.

Another theory suggested that the murder might have been part of a wider pattern of killings, with Dando being the victim of a more extensive criminal network. However, no other similar murders had occurred in the same area, making this theory unlikely.

4. ***The Role of the Media***: As a prominent media figure, Jill Dando's murder attracted significant media attention, which made the investigation all the more challenging. Journalists and the public alike were eager for answers, and the high-profile nature of the case led to intense pressure on the police to solve it quickly. The media played a key role in keeping the case in the public eye, but at times, the relentless speculation and rumors fueled confusion and made the investigation more complicated.

Theories and Speculation

While the case remains unsolved, several theories about the identity of the killer and the motive behind the crime have circulated over the years:

1. ***Professional Hit***: Some have speculated that Dando's murder was the result of a professional hit, potentially ordered by someone who had a grudge against her. This theory suggests that the killer may have been hired by an individual who had been wronged or

damaged by Jill's work on *Crimewatch* or her public persona.

2. ***A Stalker***: Another theory is that Jill was targeted by a stalker, someone who had been watching her for some time and harbored an obsession with her. Barry George, who was later wrongly convicted, had made strange comments about Dando prior to her murder, leading some to speculate that he might have been her stalker. However, this theory remains inconclusive.

3. ***Random Act of Violence***: Some believe that Jill's murder was the result of a random act of violence, possibly committed by someone who had no personal connection to her but decided to kill her for reasons that remain unknown. This theory would suggest that the killer simply saw an opportunity and took it, without any prior intention to harm Dando.

4. ***Gang or Criminal Motive***: Another theory posits that Jill's murder was somehow linked to organized crime or a criminal enterprise. This theory is less widely supported but suggests that Jill may have inadvertently crossed paths with dangerous individuals in her career, which led to her becoming a target.

Ongoing Investigation

Jill Dando's murder remains unsolved, despite numerous investigations, arrests, and theories. The case continues to intrigue the public, and in 2020, a new investigation was launched in an attempt to identify the true killer. However, despite the best efforts of the police, the case has not moved forward significantly.

In the years since her death, Jill Dando has been remembered as one of the UK's most beloved television presenters, and her tragic murder has left a void in British broadcasting. Her family, friends, and colleagues continue to seek justice for her death, but the mystery of who killed Jill Dando remains unsolved to this day.

Sources

1. "Jill Dando Murder: The Case That Still Haunts Britain," BBC News, 2021.
2. "The Barry George Trial: An Overview," The Guardian, 2008.
3. "The Murder of Jill Dando: Unsolved Mystery," The Independent, 2019.
4. "Jill Dando's Murder: New Clues Emerge," The Times, 2020.
5. "The Mystery of Jill Dando's Murder," Crime + Investigation, 2021.

Case-13 The Case of the Lady of the Dunes – 1974, USA

"A woman found murdered on a Massachusetts beach with no identity, and over 40 years later, the mystery remains unsolved."

Discovery of the Body

The Lady of the Dunes is the name given to an unidentified woman whose body was discovered on July 26, 1974, in the dunes of Provincetown, Massachusetts. She was found by a group of local children who were walking through the sand dunes near Race Point Beach. The discovery was chilling: the woman's lifeless body was sprawled out in the sand, partially covered, and in a state of disarray. She had been violently murdered, and yet, no one knew her name.

The body was badly decomposed, but investigators quickly realized that the woman's death had not been an accident or a natural death. There were several peculiarities that made her case stand out. She had been bludgeoned and strangled, with an object thought to be a piece of cloth used to strangle her. However, despite the brutality of the crime, there were no signs of sexual assault, and nothing of value appeared to have been stolen from her. These facts led authorities to believe that the crime was not committed in a fit of rage but was a carefully planned act of violence.

What shocked the investigators even more was the absence of any identifying information about the woman. No identification, no purse, and no personal items were found near her body. Additionally, there were no obvious clues pointing to who she might have been or why she had been murdered in such a manner.

The Victim's Description

The woman was described as being in her mid-30s, standing about 5 feet 6 inches tall, with light brown or auburn hair, and wearing a distinctive blue bandana. She was dressed in a pair of tan slacks and a shirt, and her body was found with her hands tied behind her back with a pair of shoelaces. It was clear from the nature of her clothing and her appearance that she had not been living in the area long.

Her distinctive appearance—along with the fact that she had been so carefully arranged—led investigators to believe that she was not a local to Provincetown. It was suspected that the woman had either been passing through or was visiting the area. But who she was, where she came from, and why she had been killed remained a mystery.

The cause of death was later determined to be blunt force trauma to the head and strangulation. In addition to these injuries, it was also revealed that she had been murdered sometime in the late spring or early summer of 1974, based on the state of decomposition of her body.

Theories and Investigation

The investigation into the Lady of the Dunes' death began almost immediately, but leads were scarce. A few initial theories about the identity of the woman and the motive behind the murder emerged, but they were eventually ruled out or disproven.

1. ***Theories About Her Identity***: Despite the best efforts of law enforcement, the Lady of the Dunes' identity remained elusive for decades. Numerous attempts to match her physical description with missing persons reports from around the country yielded no results. Investigators consulted with FBI profilers and other experts, hoping for any clues that could lead to her identification, but these efforts failed to produce concrete results.

In 1975, a composite sketch of the woman was released to the public, which led to several tips and possible leads. However, none of these proved to be fruitful. Over time, the case grew cold, and the Lady of the Dunes became a nameless victim in the long history of unsolved murder mysteries.

2. ***The Role of the Local Community***: The close-knit nature of Provincetown led many people in the area to become deeply involved in the case, both in hopes of solving the mystery and out of a desire to ensure that the woman was given the dignity of a name. Local police officers, along with the FBI, tirelessly worked

to determine who she was, but despite their efforts, the case remained a source of frustration.

One notable aspect of the case was the suggestion that the Lady of the Dunes had been involved in a love affair or relationship gone wrong. Several theories emerged, but none of them led to a clear resolution. Some believed that she might have been a part of the counterculture movement of the 1960s and 1970s, who had been traveling through Provincetown when she was murdered. Provincetown had long been a haven for artists, writers, and other free-spirited individuals, which led some to speculate that the woman may have been someone visiting the area for a brief period.

3. ***The Connection to James "Whitey" Bulger***: One of the more interesting theories about the Lady of the Dunes' murder emerged in the 1980s when a possible connection to notorious Boston mobster James "Whitey" Bulger was suggested. Bulger, who was involved in organized crime in the Boston area, was rumored to have ties to various murders throughout the city and beyond. Some speculated that the Lady of the Dunes may have had some connection to Bulger, either personally or through her association with the mob.

In 2010, the FBI investigated the possibility that Bulger had been involved in the murder, given the similarities between the Lady of the Dunes' killing and the mob-related killings that Bulger was known for. However, no direct evidence linking him to the case was ever found, and the theory was dismissed.

4. ***Other Theories***: Other theories about the Lady of the Dunes' death have centered on the possibility that she had been involved in drug smuggling or was the victim of a random act of violence. The lack of personal belongings and the violent nature of her death suggested that she might have been involved in illegal activities or that she had been in the wrong place at the wrong time.

Some have speculated that she may have been killed by a serial killer, pointing to the similarities between her case and other unsolved murders of the time. Others have suggested that she may have been a victim of human trafficking or had been murdered by a person with a personal vendetta.

The Breakthrough: DNA Evidence

For years, the Lady of the Dunes remained unidentified, and the case continued to grow colder. However, in recent years, advancements in forensic technology brought new hope to solving the mystery. In 2021, after more than 40 years of investigation, the case was reopened by the Provincetown Police Department, and a new team of detectives took a fresh look at the evidence.

The most significant breakthrough came when DNA analysis was applied to the remains of the Lady of the Dunes. The DNA was compared to databases of missing persons across the country, and in 2022, investigators announced a potential match to a woman named Ruth Marie Terry, who had been reported missing in 1974. Terry had disappeared from the Michigan area in the same year as the Lady of the Dunes' death, and DNA samples suggested that she may have been the victim found in Provincetown.

However, this theory is still under investigation, and as of yet, Ruth Marie Terry's connection to the Lady of the Dunes' murder has not been definitively proven. The case is still ongoing, with investigators hoping that new forensic evidence or additional leads will eventually bring closure to this long-unsolved mystery.

Conclusion

The case of the Lady of the Dunes remains one of the most haunting and perplexing unsolved murders in American history. For decades, her identity remained a mystery, and despite numerous theories and leads, her killer has yet to be identified. However, with the recent breakthrough in DNA testing, there is a renewed sense of hope that justice will eventually be served, and the Lady of the Dunes will no longer remain a nameless victim.

As the investigation continues, the case serves as a reminder of the many unsolved mysteries that exist, and the determination of law enforcement to uncover the truth, no matter how long it takes.

Sources

1. *"The Lady of the Dunes: A Mystery That's Haunted Provincetown for Decades," Boston Globe, 2021.*

2. *"The Lady of the Dunes and the Search for Ruth Marie Terry,"* NBC News, 2022.
3. *"The Mystery of the Lady of the Dunes: New Leads and DNA Breakthrough,"* FBI.gov, 2022.
4. *"James 'Whitey' Bulger and the Lady of the Dunes: Theories and Conspiracy,"* True Crime Daily, 2010.
5. *"The Lady of the Dunes: A Cold Case That Still Haunts,"* Crime Junkie Podcast, 2021.

Case-14 The Dyatlov Pass Incident – 1959, Russia

"Nine experienced hikers, found dead under mysterious circumstances in the Ural Mountains. Was it an attack, an accident, or something more sinister?"

The Tragic Discovery

In late January 1959, a group of nine hikers set out on an expedition in the remote Ural Mountains of Soviet Russia. Led by Igor Dyatlov, the group of students and recent graduates from the Ural Polytechnic Institute were experienced and well-prepared for their journey, which was planned to take them through the treacherous terrain of the northern Urals. The goal was to reach Otorten, a mountain peak located about 10 kilometers north of their last known campsite.

On February 26, the hikers were expected to return to their starting point, but they failed to arrive. Concerned, a search party was launched, and after several days, on February 27, rescuers found the hikers' abandoned tent on the slopes of the mountain. The tent, however, was strange—it was cut open from the inside, and their belongings, including shoes and warm clothing, were left behind in a disorganized and seemingly frantic manner. It was clear that something had gone terribly wrong.

Upon further investigation, the bodies of the nine hikers were discovered scattered across the surrounding area, some in varying states of undress. Several of them had severe injuries, while others appeared to have been exposed to the elements. As the case unfolded, the mystery of what had happened to the Dyatlov group grew even more chilling.

The Victims

The nine hikers were:

1. *Igor Dyatlov (Leader) – 23 years old*
2. *Yuri Doroshenko – 21 years old*
3. *Lyudmila Dubinina – 20 years old*
4. *Alexander Kolevatov – 24 years old*
5. *Viktor Zolotarev – 24 years old*
6. *Yuri Krivonischenko – 23 years old*
7. *Semyon Zolotaryov – 38 years old*
8. *Nikolai Thibeaux-Brignolle – 23 years old*
9. *Rustem Slobodin – 23 years old*

All were skilled hikers, experienced with the conditions they were facing, and none had ever expressed any concerns about the trek. The group had spent time preparing for the journey, obtaining proper equipment, and discussing their route before they left.

The Scene at the Campsite

Upon examining the campsite, the investigators discovered the tent in a highly unusual state. The tent had been slashed open from the inside with a knife, suggesting that the hikers had hastily cut their way out. What was perplexing, however, was that the hikers had fled the tent without their shoes, coats, or other necessary gear, even though temperatures outside were extremely cold—about -25°C (-13°F). Their tracks led away from the tent, suggesting they had run in a state of panic, with some of them apparently barefoot.

At the base of the mountain, rescuers discovered the bodies of the hikers scattered in various locations, some of them huddled together, as if seeking shelter from an unseen threat. In addition to the lack of clothing and shoes, investigators discovered that some of the victims had suffered severe, unexplained injuries, while others had injuries that were entirely inconsistent with what might be expected from a typical hiking accident.

The Injuries

The nature of the injuries sustained by the hikers was one of the most puzzling aspects of the Dyatlov Pass Incident. Of the nine hikers, four had sustained major injuries, including fractured skulls and broken ribs, but strangely, there were no external signs of violence or cuts on their bodies. The injuries appeared to have been caused by a massive force, and in some cases, the bones were broken in ways that were inconsistent with a fall or an accident.

One of the most disturbing findings was the body of **Lyudmila Dubinina**, whose eyes had been gouged out, and her tongue was missing. Her injuries were particularly gruesome, leading some to speculate that her death involved some form of ritualistic violence. However, no traces of the missing organs were ever found, and there was no evidence of foul play or external injuries to suggest an assault.

Additionally, several of the victims had radiation on their clothing, which would later be a subject of much debate. The presence of radiation was highly unusual for hikers, and some suggested that it indicated the hikers had been exposed to some sort of radioactive substance. This sparked further speculation about the cause of the incident.

Theories Behind the Mystery

The cause of the Dyatlov Pass Incident remains one of the most enduring mysteries in the history of Soviet and Russian expeditions. Over the years, many theories have emerged to explain what happened to the Dyatlov group. These theories range from natural phenomena to more speculative and sinister explanations.

1. ***Avalanche Theory***: The most widely accepted theory is that the group was caught in an avalanche. Proponents of this theory suggest that the hikers were surprised by the avalanche, which caused them to panic and flee the tent. The injuries sustained by the hikers, particularly the severe chest and head injuries, are believed to be consistent with the force of an avalanche. Some also suggest that the hikers may have been disoriented or buried under the snow, which could explain why they fled without their clothing and equipment.

2. ***Infrasound Theory***: Another theory involves infrasound, which refers to sound waves that are too low in frequency for the human ear to hear. Some researchers have suggested that a weather phenomenon in the area, combined with the specific topography of the pass, may have created infrasound, which could induce panic and irrational behavior in people. The theory argues that the hikers could have been disoriented and frightened by the sound waves, leading them to flee the tent in a state of hysteria.

3. ***Military Test Theory***: One of the more sinister theories suggests that the Dyatlov group was accidentally exposed to a military weapons test, possibly involving a secret Soviet military experiment. Some have pointed to the presence of radiation on the hikers' clothing and the odd injuries as evidence that they were killed by some sort of covert operation or weapons test, potentially related to biological or chemical agents. This theory gained traction because the area was known to be used for military testing at the time.

4. ***Yeti/Paranormal Theories***: In the years following the incident, some have speculated that the hikers were attacked by a Yeti or some other unknown creature. This theory, though widely dismissed by experts, has become part of the folklore surrounding the incident. Others have suggested paranormal explanations, such as alien involvement or a supernatural event, but there is no evidence to support these ideas.

5. ***Human Foul Play Theory***: Some believe that one of the hikers may have become violent, possibly due to psychological issues, and attacked the others. While this theory is not widely accepted due to the lack of evidence of interpersonal conflict within the group, it has been considered by investigators.

The Soviet Investigation and Cover-up

The Soviet government launched an investigation into the Dyatlov Pass Incident, but many aspects of the investigation were either incomplete or poorly handled. Initially, the authorities closed the case with a vague explanation: "death by an unknown force." The case was classified, and for many years, little information was made available to the public. Over time, it became clear that the Soviet authorities were not eager to shed light on the details of the incident, particularly given the sensitive nature of the region and its proximity to military testing areas.

Many of the files regarding the incident were sealed, and the lack of transparency led to widespread speculation and conspiracy theories. Some researchers believe that the Soviet authorities may have intentionally covered up the true cause of the hikers' deaths, either to protect the reputation of the Soviet government or because the incident involved secret military activity.

The Reopening of the Case

The case remained unresolved for decades, but in 2019, the Russian government reopened the investigation into the Dyatlov Pass Incident. The reopening followed years of renewed interest in the case, sparked in part by the release of new information and documentary films. In 2020, the Russian authorities officially concluded that the most likely cause of the deaths was an avalanche, but many details remain unclear.

While the avalanche theory is the most accepted, questions about the unusual injuries and the presence of radiation on the hikers' clothing continue to haunt the case. The full truth behind what happened to the Dyatlov group may never be fully known, but the incident remains a chilling reminder of the dangers of the wild—and of the mysteries that continue to defy explanation.

Conclusion

The Dyatlov Pass Incident stands as one of the most enigmatic and horrifying unsolved mysteries of the 20th century. The tragic deaths of the nine hikers, along with the strange circumstances surrounding their injuries and the abandonment of their campsite, continue to puzzle experts and enthusiasts alike. While new theories continue to emerge, the case remains shrouded in mystery, leaving questions that may never be answered.

Sources

1. *"The Dyatlov Pass Incident: A Search for Answers," BBC News, 2019.*
2. *"The Dyatlov Pass: Soviet Mystery in the Ural Mountains," The New York Times, 2020.*
3. *"Dyatlov Pass Reopened: What Happened in 1959?" Russian Ministry of Internal Affairs, 2020.*
4. *"The Dyatlov Pass Incident and the Avalanche Theory," National Geographic, 2021.*
5. *"The Dyatlov Pass: Unsolved and Unforgettable," Crime Investigation Network, 2022.*

Case-15 The Killing of Ashok Jadeja – 1997, India

"A promising young businessman gunned down in broad daylight in a bustling city. What led to the brutal murder of Ashok Jadeja?"

The Incident

On the morning of January 12, 1997, Ashok Jadeja, a well-known businessman from Ahmedabad, Gujarat, was shot dead in broad daylight near his office in the busy area of C.G. Road. Jadeja, a successful entrepreneur with several commercial ventures to his name, was 38 years old at the time of his murder. His death was shocking not just because of the brazenness of the act but also because of the circumstances that surrounded it.

Ashok Jadeja was a prominent figure in the city's business community, with interests ranging from real estate to finance. He was also known for his philanthropic efforts, contributing to various social causes. However, despite his respectable public persona, Jadeja was believed to have had a controversial side—his involvement with certain underworld figures and his business dealings with a range of unsavory characters eventually became a central point of investigation.

The Day of the Murder

On the fateful morning of January 12, Ashok Jadeja was heading to his office on C.G. Road, accompanied by his driver, when a car, presumably driven by two assailants, intercepted his vehicle. At that time, Jadeja was traveling in a white Ambassador car. As the vehicles slowed down near the busy road, the assailants pulled out firearms and opened fire on Jadeja at close range. According to eyewitnesses, they shot him at least five times, targeting his chest and head, before quickly fleeing the scene.

Despite being rushed to a nearby hospital immediately after the shooting, Ashok Jadeja succumbed to his injuries. His murder was not just a blow to his family but to the entire business community in Ahmedabad, leaving many shocked and in disbelief over the targeted killing of a man who had made his mark as a respectable businessman.

Investigation and Initial Theories

The Ahmedabad police launched a massive investigation into the murder of Ashok Jadeja, which quickly became a high-profile case. Given Jadeja's reputation and his connections to various businesses, the police initially considered several possible motives for his killing, including rivalry, financial disputes, or personal enmity.

One of the earliest theories that emerged was that the murder could have been the result of a rivalry in business. Jadeja had reportedly been involved in disputes with several businessmen in the city over land deals and property transactions. According to some sources, he had conflicts with others in the real estate industry, with accusations of fraud and shady business dealings. Several individuals connected to these dealings were questioned, but no concrete evidence emerged to connect them to the crime.

Another possibility explored by the police was the involvement of the underworld. Jadeja was known to have associations with various criminals and gangsters operating in Ahmedabad and other parts of Gujarat. These ties to the criminal underworld, coupled with his rapid rise in the business world, led some to speculate that the murder was linked to a power struggle between rival criminal factions or to debts that Jadeja may have accumulated through these connections.

In the early stages of the investigation, a breakthrough came when the police discovered that the assailants were likely hired killers, operating on the instructions of someone with a vested interest in Jadeja's death. The fact that the murder had been executed in a calculated manner, with the assailants firing at point-blank range and then quickly fleeing the scene, suggested that it was a planned execution rather than a spontaneous act of violence.

Underworld Connections and Motive

As the investigation unfolded, it became increasingly clear that Ashok Jadeja's murder had deeper ties to the criminal underworld, and the motive behind the killing may have been linked to debts, extortion, and other illicit business activities. The police began to investigate Jadeja's connections to a powerful figure in Gujarat's underworld: **Shabir Memon**, a notorious gangster known for his involvement in extortion and money laundering.

Shabir Memon was believed to have had a number of high-profile associates, including businessmen, politicians, and law enforcement officers. Jadeja's name had come up in some police reports as having been involved in financial transactions that seemed to have crossed the line into illegal activities, though these were not confirmed by any hard evidence. Investigators also noted that Jadeja was known to have used his influence to settle business disputes, and some of these settlements may have involved criminal elements.

The investigation revealed that Jadeja had been the target of a series of threats from the underworld prior to his murder, some of which had been linked to extortion and debt recovery. Sources within the police force suggested that Jadeja may have refused to comply with certain demands from criminal gangs, which could have led to his assassination.

The Role of the Hitmen

In March 1997, after extensive investigation, the police arrested a group of individuals who were allegedly responsible for carrying out the murder. These individuals were found to be professional hitmen, hired by a local gangster with the purpose of eliminating Jadeja. The police identified **Salim Mistry** as the mastermind behind the plot, with several accomplices involved in the planning and execution of the crime.

Mistry, a known associate of Shabir Memon, had allegedly hired the hitmen after Jadeja had refused to pay off a significant sum of money that was owed to the underworld. Mistry and his associates had reportedly been pressuring Jadeja to settle the debt, but he had resisted, possibly leading to the escalation of tensions and, ultimately, his murder.

The hitmen confessed to their involvement, detailing how they had been paid a substantial sum of money to carry out the killing. They revealed that they had been monitoring Jadeja's movements for several days before striking on the morning of January 12. They had carefully planned the attack, ensuring that Jadeja was killed in a way that would send a clear message to others involved in the underworld's illegal activities.

The Arrests and Aftermath

Following the arrests of the hitmen, the investigation revealed that the conspiracy to murder Ashok Jadeja was much larger than initially believed. Several others were implicated in the plot, including key members of Shabir Memon's criminal organization. The police eventually arrested **Salim Mistry** and charged him with masterminding the murder, along with the hitmen and others who were involved in the execution of the plan.

However, despite the arrests and confessions, the investigation raised serious concerns about the extent of corruption within law enforcement and the criminal underworld. Some believed that key figures in Jadeja's life, including those who had helped him with business dealings, had also played a role in facilitating the events leading to his death.

Though the case resulted in convictions, the full extent of the motives and the network behind the murder remained unclear. Many questions surrounding Jadeja's involvement with the criminal world, his debts, and his business practices remained unanswered.

Conclusion

The killing of Ashok Jadeja in 1997 was a tragedy that shook the city of Ahmedabad and highlighted the underworld's growing influence on businesses in Gujarat at the time. While the investigation into the case led to the arrest of several individuals, the broader network of those who orchestrated the murder remained elusive for many years. The case was a stark reminder of the dangerous intersection between business, crime, and corruption, and the lengths to which some individuals will go to settle scores in the underworld.

Though justice was served to some extent with the arrests of the murderers, the true extent of Ashok Jadeja's connections and the full details of why he was targeted remain a mystery to this day.

Sources

1. *"The Ashok Jadeja Murder Case: Unveiling the Underworld Connection," Times of India, 1997.*
2. *"Gujarat: Businessman Ashok Jadeja Shot Dead," Indian Express, 1997.*
3. *"Gangster Shabir Memon and the Murder of Ashok Jadeja," The Hindu, 1997.*
4. *"Ahmedabad's Gangster Underworld: The Rise and Fall of Ashok Jadeja," Gujarat Today, 1998.*
5. *"The Execution of Ashok Jadeja: A Murder of Convenience," Crime Investigation India, 2000.*

Case-16 The Murder of Aarushi Talwar – 2008, India

"The brutal murder of a young girl, shrouded in mystery, scandal, and controversy. Who killed Aarushi Talwar?"

The Incident

On the morning of May 16, 2008, a tragic and shocking crime came to light in Noida, Uttar Pradesh, when 14-year-old Aarushi Talwar was found murdered in her bedroom. Aarushi, the only child of Rajesh and Nupur Talwar, a well-known dentist couple, was discovered with her throat slit and a deep head injury. Her body was found by the family's domestic help, who had gone to wake her up for school.

What made the situation even more disturbing was that Aarushi's body was discovered in a locked room. Her bedroom door was found to be locked from the inside, with no clear way for the perpetrator to escape. To make matters worse, the murder was compounded by the subsequent discovery of the body of the domestic help, Hemraj Banjade, found on the terrace of the Talwar residence the following day. Hemraj had been a trusted servant of the family for several years. Both Aarushi and Hemraj's murders were initially believed to be linked.

The immediate discovery of the crime shocked the family, the local community, and the country. What followed was one of India's most high-profile and controversial murder investigations that would span over a decade, attracting widespread media attention and public debate. The investigation into the murder of Aarushi Talwar soon became clouded with multiple theories, accusations, and contradictory findings, creating a narrative filled with suspicion and confusion.

Investigation Begins

The Noida Police quickly initiated an investigation, focusing on the possibility of a domestic angle to the murder. Initial suspicions were placed on the family's domestic help, Hemraj, who was believed to have been in the house the night before Aarushi's body was discovered. However, when Hemraj's body was found, the case took a more complicated turn, as it became evident that there was more to the murder than initially thought.

At the outset, the police speculated that a possible sexual assault could have been a motive for the murder, as Aarushi's body was found in a compromising position. A subsequent investigation of the crime scene revealed signs of struggle in Aarushi's bedroom, with the police finding evidence of bloodstains and signs of forced entry into her room.

The investigation was marred by early missteps. The Noida Police were criticized for failing to secure the crime scene, for mishandling evidence, and for leaking information to the press. One of the key blunders occurred when a police officer, unaware of the gravity of the case, cleaned Aarushi's bedroom before forensic experts had arrived, potentially destroying crucial evidence. As the investigation progressed, the case grew increasingly murky, with authorities and media outlets offering conflicting theories about who could be responsible for the crime.

The First Arrest: Rajesh and Nupur Talwar

Amid the confusion, the focus of the investigation shifted towards Aarushi's parents, Rajesh and Nupur Talwar. On May 23, just days after the murder, the Talwars were arrested for the murder of their daughter and domestic help. The police claimed that the couple had orchestrated the murders in a fit of rage, motivated by suspicions of an extramarital affair between Aarushi and Hemraj. According to the police, Rajesh Talwar allegedly found his daughter in a compromising situation with Hemraj and murdered them both in a fit of rage.

However, the arrest of the Talwars was met with widespread public backlash and confusion. The police were criticized for arresting the parents without strong evidence, and many questioned the credibility of the police's theory. Despite the lack of solid proof, the case against Rajesh and Nupur Talwar seemed to be built on circumstantial evidence, such as the fact that the murder had occurred within their house and that they were among the last people to have seen Aarushi alive.

The Talwars maintained their innocence throughout the investigation and their subsequent trial. They argued that they had been framed by the police, who had failed to gather any meaningful evidence against them. The case against them was based largely on the premise of parental suspicion, with no direct evidence linking them to the crime.

The CBI Investigation and Inconsistent Findings

In 2009, amid mounting pressure, the Central Bureau of Investigation (CBI), India's premier investigation agency, took over the case. Initially, the CBI seemed to support the theory that the murders were committed by the Talwars, with its investigators citing inconsistencies in the couple's statements. However, as the investigation progressed, the CBI struggled to build a solid case.

The CBI also explored multiple other theories, including the involvement of the family's domestic help, Hemraj, whom they initially suspected but could not conclusively link to the murder. At one point, the CBI suggested that a possible outsider could have committed the crime, citing the lack of forced entry into the Talwar home. A mysterious man was even identified as a possible suspect, but the leads went nowhere.

The CBI's investigation was further complicated by a series of contradictory findings. For example, the forensic report revealed that the murder weapon, which appeared to be a sharp object such as a golf club or a surgical instrument, was never found. Despite the lack of crucial evidence, the investigation continued, with each new theory seeming to contradict the last.

The Trial and Conviction

The case against Rajesh and Nupur Talwar reached the courtroom in 2012. The couple's trial garnered significant media attention, with the prosecution focusing on circumstantial evidence, including the theory that Rajesh Talwar was the murderer. The defense argued that there was no direct evidence linking the Talwars to the murders, and they questioned the handling of the investigation by the police and the CBI.

In November 2013, after months of hearings, the special CBI court in Ghaziabad convicted Rajesh and Nupur Talwar for the murders of Aarushi and Hemraj. The court sentenced them to life imprisonment, finding them guilty of both murders. However, the trial and subsequent conviction were met with widespread criticism, with many legal experts arguing that the case against the Talwars was circumstantial at best and that the evidence was insufficient to support a conviction.

The Talwars appealed the verdict, and in 2017, the Allahabad High Court acquitted them, citing the lack of conclusive evidence against the couple. The court ruled that the prosecution had failed to prove its case beyond a reasonable doubt, and the Talwars were released from prison after serving four years.

The acquittal was hailed as a victory for the Talwars, but it also left many unanswered questions about the murder. The case remains unresolved, with no one having been definitively convicted for the deaths of Aarushi and Hemraj.

Conclusion

The murder of Aarushi Talwar remains one of India's most baffling and controversial cases. The investigation was plagued by missteps, inconsistencies, and shifting theories, and the trial generated intense media scrutiny. While Rajesh and Nupur Talwar were acquitted in 2017, the true identity of the killer—or killers—has never been determined.

The case has left a deep scar on Indian society, particularly on the Talwar family, who continue to maintain their innocence despite the court's decision. The Aarushi Talwar case highlights the challenges of high-profile investigations and the importance of a fair and thorough investigation to uncover the truth.

The question remains: who killed Aarushi Talwar and Hemraj Banjade? The answer may never come, but the mystery surrounding the case continues to haunt the public imagination.

Sources

1. *"Aarushi Talwar Murder: The Untold Story," NDTV, 2008.*
2. *"The Aarushi Talwar Case: A Legal Perspective," The Times of India, 2013.*
3. *"CBI's Investigation in the Aarushi Talwar Case," The Hindu, 2009.*
4. *"The Trial of Rajesh and Nupur Talwar," India Today, 2017.*

5. "Aarushi Talwar Murder: The Case that Stunned India," India Express, 2017.

Case-17 The Phantom of Heilbronn – 1993–2009, Germany

"A mystery that spanned over 16 years and involved a series of chilling unsolved crimes. Who was the elusive 'Phantom of Heilbronn'?"

The Incident

The 'Phantom of Heilbronn' was a name given to an elusive and unknown serial killer whose crimes terrorized Germany over a span of 16 years, from 1993 to 2009. The case was characterized by a mysterious pattern of killings, robberies, and other violent acts, all of which seemed to be connected by one central clue: DNA evidence. The killer's DNA was found at numerous crime scenes, but despite extensive investigation, the identity of the killer remained unknown for years.

The crimes that were attributed to the Phantom began in 1993, when a series of robberies and violent attacks started to be linked together. The initial crimes were relatively minor, but by the late 1990s, the Phantom's crimes began to escalate, involving the murder of police officers and others. The most infamous of the Phantom's crimes was the murder of two police officers, Michèle Kiesewetter and her partner, during a routine traffic stop in Heilbronn in 2007. The killing marked the peak of the Phantom's violent spree, and it was this murder that brought the case to the attention of the German police and the public.

The DNA Evidence

One of the most striking features of the Phantom of Heilbronn case was the recurring appearance of the same DNA at multiple crime scenes. The police found this DNA at various locations linked to the killer's crimes, including a series of robberies, rapes, and murders. The DNA was consistently found on items such as discarded gloves, objects at the crime scene, and even directly on the victims. Over time, investigators began to believe that they were looking for a single individual whose DNA had been left behind at these crime scenes.

As the years passed, the police and forensic teams worked tirelessly to track down the killer based on this genetic evidence. Investigators compiled a vast database of criminal DNA profiles from individuals with prior offenses, hoping to match the Phantom's DNA with someone already in their system. However, every attempt at matching the DNA to known criminals failed. The case seemed to be at a standstill, and frustration grew among law enforcement officials as the Phantom continued to elude capture.

By 2007, the case had taken on a high-profile status, with the murder of two police officers intensifying the public and media's interest in the case. The investigators remained puzzled, unable to make any significant breakthroughs.

A Break in the Case: The Revelation

The breakthrough came in 2009, when investigators finally discovered an extraordinary and unexpected twist in the case. It was revealed that the DNA found at the crime scenes did not belong to a suspect at all, but rather to a female police officer who had worked on the case.

The female officer, whose name was never publicly disclosed, had unknowingly contaminated evidence during her work in the laboratory. The officer was part of the team handling DNA samples collected from the various crime scenes over the years. The traces of her DNA had transferred to the evidence through her gloves or during the processing of samples, leading investigators to mistakenly believe that the DNA belonged to the killer.

Once the contamination was discovered, the police realized that the 'Phantom of Heilbronn' did not exist. The entire case, which had been investigated for over 16 years, was the result of a misunderstanding and a series of unfortunate events. The DNA that had been collected from the crime scenes was never linked to any one person but rather to the officer who had worked with the evidence. The realization that the supposed serial killer was a product of laboratory contamination shocked both law enforcement and the public.

Impact on the Investigation

The revelation of DNA contamination by the officer completely dismantled the theory of the "Phantom of Heilbronn." It also left the police grappling with questions about the accuracy and reliability of forensic science in criminal investigations. For years, the German police had believed they were dealing with a sophisticated and elusive criminal who had managed to evade justice. However, the true cause of the confusion was human error.

The contamination not only explained why the DNA appeared at so many crime scenes, but it also cast doubt on the many conclusions drawn by law enforcement in the case. The police had conducted numerous investigations and used the DNA evidence to rule out suspects, even while unknowingly working with flawed information. The discovery led to the re-evaluation of all the crimes linked to the Phantom and revealed that many of them might have been unrelated to the same individual.

In the aftermath of the scandal, German authorities acknowledged the mistakes made during the investigation. The police officer involved in the contamination was deeply remorseful, and the forensic practices in the country were re-examined to prevent similar issues in the future. Despite the embarrassment caused by the mix-up, authorities stressed that the error was not intentional and that it was the result of a series of unfortunate events, compounded by the limitations of forensic science.

Conclusion

The 'Phantom of Heilbronn' case is one of the most bizarre and baffling criminal mysteries in modern history. What was initially believed to be a long-running serial killer case turned out to be an unfortunate mix-up caused by DNA contamination. The revelation that the DNA belonged to a female officer rather than a criminal rocked the world of forensic science and raised questions about the reliability of evidence collected in criminal investigations.

While the mystery of the Phantom was resolved in 2009, the case serves as a stark reminder of the potential pitfalls of forensic science and the importance of maintaining rigorous standards in criminal investigations. The 'Phantom of Heilbronn' became a cautionary tale in the world of law enforcement, highlighting how even the most sophisticated investigative methods can be flawed due to human error.

Though the killer was never found, the case remains an example of how science and technology, while invaluable tools, can sometimes create more confusion than clarity if not handled with care and precision.

Sources

1. *"The Phantom of Heilbronn: The Case of the Elusive Serial Killer," The Guardian, 2009.*
2. *"How DNA Contamination Created a Fictional Killer," The Times, 2009.*
3. *"The Phantom of Heilbronn: Germany's Most Mysterious Serial Killer Case," BBC News, 2009.*
4. *"A Tragic Mistake: The Phantom of Heilbronn DNA Scandal," Der Spiegel, 2009.*

Case-18 The Olof Palme Assassination – 1986, Sweden

"The murder of Sweden's Prime Minister remains one of the most enigmatic political assassinations of the 20th century. Who killed Olof Palme?"

The Incident

On the night of February 28, 1986, Olof Palme, the Prime Minister of Sweden, was shot dead in the streets of Stockholm. His assassination shocked Sweden, a nation known for its political stability and peace. Palme, who had been in office for over a decade, was walking home with his wife, Lisbeth, after a night at the cinema when the gunman approached them from behind. The assailant fired two shots—one of which struck Palme in the back, killing him instantly. His wife, Lisbeth, was unharmed. The killer fled the scene without saying a word, disappearing into the cold Stockholm night.

Despite an extensive investigation by Swedish authorities and worldwide media attention, the case remained unsolved for decades. Numerous theories about the identity of the killer and the motive behind the assassination circulated, but no one was ever convicted of Palme's murder. Over the years, the case became one of the most famous unsolved political assassinations in modern history, leaving Sweden—and the world—grappling with the question: who killed Olof Palme?

The Investigation Begins

The initial response from the Swedish police was swift and well-coordinated. They quickly secured the area surrounding the crime scene and launched a massive manhunt to track down the killer. However, despite initial hopes that the case would be quickly solved, there were no immediate breakthroughs.

The investigation into the murder was complicated by a number of factors. For one, there were no reliable witnesses who could provide a description of the shooter. Lisbeth Palme, the prime minister's wife, was too shaken and traumatized to offer a detailed account of the events. The police had little physical evidence to go on. While they did find two shell casings at the scene, the gun itself was never recovered, and no clear traces of the killer were left behind.

Early on, investigators faced a number of false leads and theories. Some suggested that the assassination was politically motivated due to Palme's outspoken stance on international issues, including his criticism of the Vietnam War and his support for the Palestinian cause. Others speculated that it was linked to domestic terrorism, organized crime, or even personal grievances.

Despite the lack of solid evidence, the Swedish police persisted with their investigation, interviewing hundreds of potential witnesses and persons of interest. But each lead turned out to be a dead end.

The Theories and Suspects

Over the years, several theories emerged about who was behind the murder of Olof Palme. Among the most prominent suspects were:

1. ***The Swedish Extreme Right***: Some believed that Palme's policies, particularly his support for international peace efforts and his criticism of the United States during the Cold War, made him a target for far-right extremists. A popular theory suggested that a far-right group may have orchestrated the assassination as retaliation for Palme's political stances. Several people linked to far-right organizations were investigated, but no direct evidence ever tied them to the crime.

2. ***The Kurdish Connection***: Another theory pointed to the Kurdish separatist group, the PKK (Kurdistan Workers' Party), which had an ongoing conflict with Turkey. Palme had been an outspoken advocate for Kurdish rights, and some believed that the PKK might have seen him as a threat due to his international influence. However, despite a number of arrests and investigations into Kurdish groups, no conclusive evidence was found to support this theory.

3. ***The Police Officer Theory***: In the years following the murder, there were persistent rumors that the killer could have been a police officer who had access to sensitive information about Palme's movements. One suspect, a man named Christer Pettersson, was arrested

in 1988 based on the claim that he resembled a police sketch of the killer. Pettersson was convicted in 1989, but the verdict was overturned on appeal due to lack of evidence, and he was never retried. His involvement remains a point of debate among investigators and conspiracy theorists.

4. ***The Lone Gunman****:* One of the most widely accepted theories, though still unproven, is that Palme was assassinated by a lone gunman acting on personal motivations. Some believe the killer had a personal vendetta against the Prime Minister and decided to act on it in an impulsive act of violence. However, without any clear suspects or motives, this theory remains speculative.

The Breakthrough: New Investigations and Closing the Case

In 2019, after over three decades of unsuccessful investigations, Swedish prosecutors announced they would close the case and formally end the investigation into Palme's murder. The case had gone through numerous stages of investigation and had been re-opened multiple times with new theories and suspects, but none had been conclusively linked to the crime.

The Swedish police were able to rule out many of the earlier suspects, but they could never definitively identify the murderer. As time went on, the investigation was further complicated by the fact that many key witnesses had either died or could no longer recall important details from the night of the murder.

Despite years of effort, Palme's killer remained a ghost. The case was ultimately closed without anyone being arrested or charged for the crime, leaving many questions unanswered. Still, for those who followed the case, the haunting mystery of who killed Olof Palme remained one of the most enduring enigmas of modern crime history.

The Lasting Impact

The assassination of Olof Palme had a profound impact on Sweden, both politically and socially. Palme was one of the country's most influential and charismatic leaders, and his sudden and brutal death sent shockwaves through the Swedish political landscape. His assassination also created a sense of unease in Sweden, a country that had prided itself on being a peaceful and stable democracy.

Over the years, the case has remained a source of national trauma and intrigue, with countless theories, documentaries, and books being written about the murder. While the police have closed the investigation, the identity of Palme's killer remains a mystery, and the impact of his death on Swedish politics and society continues to be felt to this day.

The unsolved nature of Olof Palme's assassination is a reminder of the complex and often unpredictable world of political violence. Though many suspects have been investigated and theories proposed, the truth behind the murder of Olof Palme remains as elusive as it was on that fateful night in February 1986.

Sources

1. "Olof Palme: A Prime Minister's Murder Still Unsolved," BBC News, 2019.
2. "The Unsolved Murder of Olof Palme," The Guardian, 2018.
3. "Olof Palme: Murder and Mystery," New York Times, 2017.
4. "Olof Palme Assassination: A Timeline of Events," Swedish Police Report, 2019.
5. "The Case of Olof Palme: Investigating the Assassin," Swedish National Archives, 2017.

Case-19 The Murder of Sister Abhaya – 1992, India

"The murder of Sister Abhaya remains one of the most perplexing and tragic criminal cases in India, a case filled with mystery, controversy, and years of unanswered questions."

The Incident

On March 27, 1992, Sister Abhaya, a 21-year-old Catholic nun, was found dead in the well of a convent hostel in Kottayam, Kerala. The convent was run by the Missionaries of Jesus, a Catholic order, and was situated near the St. Pius X College. Sister Abhaya, a novice at the convent, had been living there for several months, diligently pursuing her religious training and studies.

Sister Abhaya's body was discovered early in the morning by a fellow nun, who noticed that she was missing from the dormitory. A search was launched, and her body was eventually found in the convent's well, located in the kitchen area. Her death was initially treated as a suicide, but there were several inconsistencies in the evidence, and suspicions soon arose that her death was not as simple as it appeared.

The well, where her body was discovered, was not far from the kitchen, and the circumstances surrounding her death were highly suspicious. A postmortem examination revealed that

Sister Abhaya had been murdered—she had been hit on the head with a blunt object, which caused blunt force trauma to her skull. There were no signs of drowning, indicating that her body had been placed in the well after she was killed.

Given the nature of the case, the local police quickly reclassified the death as a homicide, and an investigation was launched. However, despite their efforts, the investigation faced several obstacles. There was no clear motive, and the evidence seemed to point in multiple directions, making it difficult for investigators to establish a definitive cause for Sister Abhaya's tragic death.

Early Investigation and Suspicion

The first phase of the investigation was marred by the lack of clarity surrounding the motive behind the murder. Sister Abhaya was described by her fellow nuns and those who knew her as a devout and kind individual, with no known enemies. She had been in the convent for over a year and had never given any indication of any personal strife or external threats. Her death, therefore, seemed to be both puzzling and senseless.

Initially, the police did not focus on any specific individuals and tried to reconstruct the events surrounding the murder. A key lead came from the testimony of a few nuns who reported hearing strange noises from the convent's kitchen area during the night of the murder. However, the lack of physical evidence and the initial theories that the death might have been a suicide or an accidental fall into the well led to confusion.

During this period, many questions arose about the role of the members of the convent, especially given the tight-knit nature of the religious community. There was no clear answer to how Sister Abhaya could have ended up in the well, and why she would have been murdered. Some began speculating that the case may have involved members of the clergy, particularly after inconsistencies in the testimonies of some of the convent's staff came to light.

Breakthrough in the Case: The Role of Father Kottoor and Sister Sephy

For years, the case seemed to stall, and no significant progress was made. However, in 2008, the investigation was revitalized, and the case took a dramatic turn. The Kerala Police Special Investigation Team (SIT), which had been tasked with re-investigating the murder, unearthed new evidence pointing to two members of the convent: Father Kottoor and Sister Sephy, both of whom had been closely associated with Sister Abhaya.

According to the new investigation, it was revealed that Father Kottoor, a priest who had a key role in the convent, and Sister Sephy had been involved in an illicit relationship. It was alleged that on the night of the murder, Sister Abhaya had discovered their secret affair. Fearing that the affair would be exposed and their positions within the convent would be jeopardized, Father Kottoor and Sister Sephy allegedly decided to silence her.

The investigators hypothesized that Sister Abhaya had witnessed the two engaged in the compromising situation, and in a panic, Father Kottoor and Sister Sephy allegedly conspired to murder her. They reportedly struck her on the head with a blunt object, killing her. Afterward, they allegedly staged the scene by placing her body in the well, hoping to make it appear as though she had committed suicide.

The involvement of Father Kottoor and Sister Sephy was further supported by a series of circumstantial evidence, including their suspicious behavior following the murder, conflicting statements about their whereabouts, and the discovery of incriminating materials related to the case. However, it wasn't until 2008 that the police were able to make significant progress in formally linking them to the crime.

The Legal Battle and Convictions

The case went through a protracted legal process. In 2008, after more than a decade of investigations and legal proceedings, Father Kottoor and Sister Sephy were arrested and charged with murder, conspiracy, and destruction of evidence. The case went through several trials, and in 2018, the Kerala High Court found both of them guilty and sentenced them to life imprisonment.

However, the case did not end with this conviction. Over the years, there had been consistent speculation that the investigation was flawed, and some argued that there were political or institutional pressures that had influenced the case. Despite the convictions, many continued to question the true motives behind Sister Abhaya's murder and whether the real culprits were brought to justice.

The long and complicated case has left many unanswered questions, with some continuing to believe that the full truth has not yet come to light. Despite the convictions, there is still lingering public doubt over the case, leading to calls for further investigation into the possible involvement of others.

Impact on Indian Society and the Church

The murder of Sister Abhaya, and the subsequent revelations surrounding her death, had a significant impact on both Indian society and the Church. It exposed deep flaws within the Catholic Church in India, particularly in the way it handled allegations of abuse and misconduct. The case also drew attention to the challenges faced by women within religious institutions, as it became evident that Sister Abhaya's attempts to expose corruption and misconduct within the Church may have played a role in her death.

For the Church, the case highlighted the need for greater transparency, accountability, and reform in its internal affairs. The conviction of Father Kottoor and Sister Sephy was a somber reminder of the risks posed by secrecy and abuse of power within religious organizations. The murder left many wondering about the hidden lives of those who are trusted with sacred responsibilities and how a culture of silence could lead to tragic consequences.

Conclusion

The murder of Sister Abhaya remains one of India's most tragic and controversial cases, a case that transcends the bounds of mere criminality and speaks to broader issues of morality, power, and the vulnerabilities of women in institutions. Despite the conviction of Father Kottoor and Sister Sephy, the case continues to haunt many, especially those who knew Sister Abhaya as a young woman full of promise and potential. Her death represents a complex intersection of crime, religion, and the quest for justice, making it a case that will be remembered for generations to come.

Sources

1. "The Murder of Sister Abhaya: A Timeline," The Hindu, 2018.
2. "Father Kottoor, Sister Sephy Convicted in Murder of Sister Abhaya," Times of India, 2018.
3. "Sister Abhaya Case: The Quest for Justice," Kerala Police Investigation Report, 2008.
4. "The Case of Sister Abhaya: Legal and Social Implications," Indian Law Journal, 2019.
5. "The Tragic Murder of Sister Abhaya," The New Indian Express, 2008.

Case-20 The Death of Natalie Wood – 1981, USA

"The tragic death of Natalie Wood remains one of Hollywood's most enduring mysteries, shrouded in intrigue and speculation. Despite numerous investigations and conflicting accounts, the truth behind her untimely demise on a cold November night remains elusive."

The Incident

On the evening of November 28, 1981, actress Natalie Wood, known for her iconic roles in *West Side Story*, *Rebel Without a Cause*, and *Splendor in the Grass*, was found dead off the coast of Catalina Island in California. She was 43 years old. The circumstances surrounding her death have been the subject of intense scrutiny for over four decades, with theories ranging from accidental drowning to murder.

At the time of her death, Natalie Wood had been aboard the *Splendour*, a yacht owned by her husband, actor Robert Wagner. Also aboard the yacht was Christopher Walken, a co-star from Wood's latest film, *Brainstorm*. According to the official reports, Wood and Wagner had been drinking heavily on the night of her death, and a quarrel between them reportedly occurred before Wood was found in the water.

Wood's body was discovered by the yacht's captain, Dennis Davern, who had heard a noise and went on deck to investigate. She was found floating in the water, wearing a nightgown, with her face submerged. No signs of physical injury were noted, but it was clear that she had drowned. The autopsy report indicated that she had suffered bruising on her body, but the exact cause of her death remained uncertain.

Initially, the death was ruled an accidental drowning, but the circumstances of Wood's death raised questions that would remain unanswered for years.

Early Investigation and the Official Explanation

At first, the Los Angeles County Sheriff's Department treated Wood's death as an accident. The report stated that Wood had tried to leave the yacht in a small dinghy, possibly to return to shore, but the dinghy became untethered, and Wood fell into the cold waters of the Pacific Ocean. The investigation suggested that she was likely intoxicated, which contributed to her inability to survive.

However, there were inconsistencies in the testimonies from those who had been aboard the yacht that night. Captain Dennis Davern, who had been aboard the yacht during the events, initially claimed that he had heard Wood screaming, but in later interviews, he revealed that he had not been entirely truthful in his initial statements. Furthermore, Robert Wagner's behavior during the time leading up to the discovery of Wood's body raised further suspicions.

Wagner had allegedly waited several hours before notifying authorities of his wife's disappearance, which was odd given the gravity of the situation. Wagner later admitted to having a heated argument with Wood that night, but he claimed that it

136

was not violent and that he was unaware of her disappearance until it was too late.

The failure of Wagner and Walken to immediately report Wood's disappearance or attempt to rescue her, combined with conflicting statements from the crew, prompted many to question whether there was more to the story than an accident.

Theories of Murder and the Role of Robert Wagner

As time passed, the official version of Natalie Wood's death began to unravel. New theories started to surface, with some suggesting that Wood had been murdered, and that Robert Wagner, her husband, was somehow involved. These theories were fueled by Wagner's inconsistent statements, his reluctance to cooperate with the authorities, and the mysterious circumstances surrounding the night of her death.

One theory posited that Wagner and Wood had fought violently, possibly over her alleged infidelity with Christopher Walken. According to this theory, Wagner's jealousy and anger over the situation could have led him to push his wife into the water, either intentionally or in a fit of rage. Some speculated that the argument escalated to the point where Wagner, in a moment of blind rage, may have attacked Wood.

The idea of foul play was further strengthened by the lack of concrete evidence to support the accidental drowning theory. Despite multiple investigations, there was never any definitive proof that Wood had intentionally gotten into the water. Additionally, the bruises found on Wood's body and the fact that she was unable to swim in the rough, cold water raised questions about whether she had been conscious when she fell into the ocean.

The involvement of Christopher Walken also remained a topic of debate. While Walken was never officially a suspect, the fact that he was present on the yacht during the fatal night raised suspicions. Some believed that Walken could have been a witness to the events leading up to Wood's death, but he never provided a full explanation of what transpired that night.

Reopening the Case

Despite the early investigation, the case remained largely closed, with the death officially ruled an accident. However, in 2011, the Los Angeles County Sheriff's Department announced that it would be reopening the investigation into Wood's death, citing new evidence and renewed interest in the case.

The decision to reopen the case came after Captain Davern, who had been a key witness, publicly stated that he believed Wood's death was not an accident. In interviews with the media, Davern claimed that Wagner had been involved in a violent argument with Wood, and that he had refused to assist in the search efforts after her disappearance. According to Davern, Wagner's behavior was suspicious, and he believed that Wagner had played a role in his wife's death.

The re-investigation was also spurred by the 2009 release of the book *Goodbye Natalie, Goodbye Splendour*, co-written by Captain Davern and journalist Marti Rulli. The book detailed the events leading up to Wood's death and raised questions about Wagner's involvement. The renewed investigation focused on examining new forensic evidence, including the bruises on Wood's body and the timeline of the events.

In 2012, the Sheriff's Department announced that they had changed the classification of the case from an accidental drowning to "drowning and other undetermined factors." This decision came after experts re-examined the evidence and concluded that there were too many unanswered questions to definitively rule the death an accident.

Public Reaction and the Legacy of Natalie Wood's Death

The ongoing investigation into Natalie Wood's death has kept the mystery alive in public consciousness for over four decades. Despite the renewed investigation, no charges have ever been filed, and the case remains unsolved. The conflicting accounts from the people involved, combined with the lack of concrete evidence, mean that the true cause of Wood's death may never be fully known.

For many, the death of Natalie Wood is a symbol of the darker side of Hollywood, where secrets are often buried beneath the glitz and glamour of fame. Wood was a beloved figure, and her untimely demise has only added to her tragic legacy.

Natalie Wood's death has become a part of Hollywood lore, and theories about the events of that night continue to circulate. While some believe it was an accidental drowning, others maintain that there was foul play involved. The unanswered questions surrounding her death have left a stain on the legacy of one of the most beloved actresses of her generation.

Conclusion

The death of Natalie Wood is a case that remains unresolved, with questions that may never be answered. Her tragic end, shrouded in mystery, continues to capture the public's imagination. The involvement of Robert Wagner, Christopher Walken, and the conflicting testimonies of those involved have created a case that seems destined to remain in the annals of unsolved mysteries.

Sources

1. *"The Mysterious Death of Natalie Wood," Los Angeles Times, 1981.*
2. *"Captain Dennis Davern Speaks Out About Natalie Wood," The Hollywood Reporter, 2011.*
3. *"Natalie Wood's Death: Reopened Investigation," NBC News, 2012.*
4. *Goodbye Natalie, Goodbye Splendour by Marti Rulli and Dennis Davern, 2009.*
5. *"Natalie Wood Death: A Timeline of the Investigation," People Magazine, 2011.*

Case-21 The Killing Fields – 1980s–1990s, USA

"For nearly two decades, a vast and chilling landscape of death and mystery stretched across the United States, from Texas to California. The victims, primarily young women, disappeared without a trace, leaving behind only the haunting question: Who was responsible for the Killing Fields?"

The Discovery of the Killing Fields

In the early 1980s, the quiet, rural areas along the Gulf Coast of Texas began to attract national attention, but for all the wrong reasons. The region, known as the "Killing Fields," earned its grim reputation due to the discovery of a series of murdered young women whose bodies were found buried in a desolate, marshy area just outside of Galveston, Texas. These areas became infamous due to the high concentration of unsolved murders that seemed to have been committed over a span of several years.

It all began in 1983 when the body of a teenage girl, later identified as 15-year-old Laura Miller, was found in a field near a gas station in League City, Texas. She had been missing for several weeks, and her body showed signs of brutal violence. The discovery sparked the realization that this area of Texas might be hiding a darker truth — that a serial killer might be operating in the region.

The Killing Fields, however, were not confined to just one victim or one location. Over the next several years, more bodies began to surface — all of young women, many of whom had been sexually assaulted, and some who were found with their hands bound. It wasn't long before law enforcement officials realized they were facing a serial killer who was targeting vulnerable women across the region.

The Growing List of Victims

The first victim to be identified in connection with the Killing Fields was Laura Miller. However, as investigators began to dig deeper, more and more bodies were discovered. Between 1983 and 1991, several other young women were found in similar circumstances. Among the known victims were:

- ***Shandra Whitehead***, found in 1986. Her body was discovered in a field near the same area where Laura Miller was found, and like the others, she had been brutally murdered.
- ***Jessica Cain***, a 17-year-old girl who went missing in 1997. Her body was discovered years later, and she was found to have been buried in a remote area near the highway.
- ***Andrea Wilborn***, a 15-year-old girl, was last seen in 1988 and later discovered in the Killing Fields in 1991.
- ***Tonya Hughes***, another teenager, found dead in the same area in 1991.

The bodies were often discovered in rural or isolated areas close to the highway, and many of the victims had similar physical features: young, white or Latina women, most of whom were living in vulnerable situations. Some had been known to work in the sex trade or had been last seen in places where they could be easily preyed upon.

Authorities began to suspect that the murders were connected, but the investigation into the so-called Killing Fields was complicated by the lack of substantial evidence and the high turnover in local law enforcement. Many of the victims were initially written off as runaways or drug addicts, which made it difficult for law enforcement to take their disappearances seriously until the bodies started to pile up.

The Challenges of Investigation

As the body count increased, investigators were stymied by the lack of physical evidence. No clear pattern emerged that could point to a single killer, and the region's law enforcement agencies were overwhelmed by the scope of the investigation. Many of the victims had disappeared from different parts of Texas, and some had been found in different counties, which complicated the investigation even further.

Additionally, the authorities struggled to connect the killings to any one suspect. Various theories and suspects were proposed over the years, but none were proven to be the killer. Some of the theories included:

1. ***A Truck Driver or Traveling Serial Killer***: Because many of the victims were found in remote, rural

locations along highways, investigators began to speculate that the killer might have been a truck driver or someone who traveled regularly between cities and states. This theory was bolstered by the fact that the bodies were often found near highways, and the killer might have used these areas as "dump sites."

2. *A Local Killer*: Some investigators believed that the killer might be a local resident familiar with the area. This theory was supported by the fact that some of the victims had been found relatively close to where they had lived.

3. *A Serial Killer with a Pattern*: Experts began to suspect that the killer had developed a pattern, particularly targeting young women. They speculated that the killer might be someone who had a specific type of victim in mind, and the remote locations in which the bodies were found suggested a desire to hide the evidence.

Despite these theories, investigators were unable to find concrete evidence to lead them to a suspect. The case became one of the most notorious unsolved serial killings in Texas, and the Killing Fields remained a source of mystery for decades.

The Breakthrough and Renewed Investigation

The case of the Killing Fields remained largely unsolved until 2006, when a major breakthrough occurred. Authorities received a tip that led them to the identification of a potential suspect: **Samuel Little**, a man who had been serving a life sentence for other crimes. Little, who had been linked to several unsolved murders across the United States, had been interviewed by police regarding the Texas killings, but no direct connection had been made at the time.

In 2018, after DNA evidence linked Little to the murder of three women in California, he was convicted of multiple murders across the country. Investigators began to look into his potential involvement in the Killing Fields case, particularly in relation to the victims in Texas. Little had traveled extensively during the time period when the bodies were discovered, and his history of violence against women matched the profile of the victims found in the Killing Fields.

Although Little has not been conclusively linked to the killings in Texas, the renewed interest in his case and his involvement in several other cold cases prompted authorities to revisit the evidence. The possibility that Samuel Little may have been responsible for the murders in the Killing Fields remains an open question, but for many, his involvement in the case offers a glimmer of hope for closure.

The Enduring Mystery

Despite the renewed investigation, the question of who was behind the Killing Fields murders remains unsolved. While Samuel Little's potential involvement has added a new dimension to the case, the true identity of the killer, or killers, remains elusive. The Killing Fields murders remain one of the most haunting serial murder mysteries in American history, a tragic chapter that continues to spark debates and investigations.

The victims of the Killing Fields are often remembered as nameless faces in a long list of unsolved crimes, their deaths marking a dark period in Texas history. But as investigators continue to piece together the clues, there is hope that the killer will eventually be brought to justice.

Conclusion

The Killing Fields case is a haunting reminder of the dangers of ignoring the vulnerable and marginalized members of society. The young women who fell victim to the killer(s) deserve justice, and their families deserve closure. While the investigation continues to unfold, the true identity of the murderer(s) and the motivation behind the killings remain a mystery — a mystery that may one day be solved, but for now, the Killing Fields continue to hold their grim secrets.

Sources

1. *"The Killing Fields: Serial Murders in Texas," Texas Monthly, 1983-1991.*
2. *"Samuel Little's Possible Involvement in the Killing Fields Murders," NBC News, 2018.*
3. *"Unsolved Murders: The Killing Fields," CBS News, 2006.*
4. *"A Timeline of the Killing Fields Murders," Houston Chronicle, 2011.*
5. *"Samuel Little: The Most Prolific Serial Killer in American History," The Guardian, 2019.*

Extra Case-22 The Disappearance of Tara Calico

"A woman riding her bike through a quiet New Mexico town disappears without a trace, and nearly 35 years later, the mystery remains unsolved. The case of Tara Calico is a haunting reminder of how one moment can change a life forever."

The Last Ride

On September 20, 1988, Tara Calico, a 19-year-old college student from Belen, New Mexico, set out for her usual morning bike ride. She had a well-established routine, and on that fateful day, she was riding her bike along Highway 47, a quiet stretch of road near her home. Tara had been training for an upcoming 100-mile bike race, and this ride was meant to be part of her preparation.

She had planned to return home around noon, but when her mother, Patti Calico, returned from errands, Tara was nowhere to be found. Her bike was gone, and there were no signs of her along the road. Tara's disappearance was swift, and no one knew what had happened to her.

Her mother immediately called the police, and a search was launched. Volunteers, law enforcement, and even helicopters scoured the area, but there was no trace of Tara. It was as if she had simply vanished.

The Search and the Investigation

As the days passed, the investigation into Tara Calico's disappearance began to unravel the mystery of what might have happened. There was no indication of foul play at the scene of her disappearance, and the only clue left behind was Tara's pink bicycle. There were no signs of struggle, and the bike appeared to have been abandoned in the middle of the road.

In the initial stages of the investigation, police believed that Tara had been abducted. However, without any solid leads or witnesses, the case quickly grew cold. There were no ransom notes or phone calls demanding money, and no one had seen anything unusual in the area on the day she vanished.

For years, Tara's family would wait for answers. But it wasn't until several months later that a chilling lead would come to light — a photograph that would forever alter the course of the investigation.

The Polaroid Photograph

In June 1989, nearly a year after Tara disappeared, a disturbing development occurred. A Polaroid photo surfaced in a convenience store in the neighboring town of Alamogordo, New Mexico. The photo depicted a young woman who was bound and gagged, lying next to a man. The woman in the photo resembled Tara Calico, and the photo sent shockwaves through the investigation.

The image was taken in a car, and in the background, the distinctive yellow blanket that Tara was known to have used during her bike rides was visible. The discovery of this photograph sparked new hope that Tara might still be alive, but it also raised more questions than answers. Who took the photo? Was Tara really in it? And, if so, where was she?

The photo was handed over to the authorities, who began investigating the possibility that Tara had been abducted and was being held captive. However, despite extensive efforts to trace the origin of the Polaroid, the case remained a mystery. Forensics teams were unable to positively identify the woman in the photo as Tara, but many family members, friends, and even some law enforcement officers believed it was her.

The Investigation Continues

The search for Tara Calico continued for years, but there were no more solid leads. Over the years, the case would take many twists and turns, with investigators considering a variety of theories and potential suspects. Some believed that Tara had been abducted by someone familiar with the area, while others suspected the involvement of a stranger passing through.

There were several theories that gained traction over the years, including the possibility that Tara's disappearance was linked to the high-profile cases of missing women in the area during that time. However, no clear connections were ever made, and the investigation was plagued by dead ends.

In the early 1990s, a suspect named Henry Brown was briefly considered in connection with Tara's disappearance. Brown had been convicted of the kidnapping and murder of a young woman in Arizona and had spent time in New Mexico. However, no evidence could link him to Tara's case, and he was later cleared as a suspect.

The Possibility of Tara's Survival

In 1990, Tara's mother, Patti Calico, was contacted by a woman who claimed to have seen Tara alive in a nearby town. The woman claimed that she had seen a girl who looked exactly like Tara in a store, and the girl had been with a man. The witness reported that the girl seemed disoriented and frightened. However, this lead, like many others, proved to be inconclusive.

There were also other reports over the years from people who claimed to have seen Tara in various places across the United States, but none of these sightings could be verified. Despite these sightings, there was no confirmation that Tara had been alive after her disappearance, and the case remained an enigma.

The Return of the Polaroid

The mystery deepened when, in 1999, another Polaroid photo surfaced, similar to the one from 1989. This new photo showed a young woman who resembled Tara Calico, along with another man. The photo was taken in the same style, with the woman appearing bound and gagged. The image sparked new rumors, but again, no concrete evidence was found to prove that the woman in the photo was indeed Tara.

Despite the passage of time, the investigation into Tara Calico's disappearance continues. The case has never been officially closed, and Tara's mother, Patti, remains determined to find out what happened to her daughter. In 2006, she was still actively working with the authorities to investigate new leads and rumors that might bring closure to the case.

Theories and Speculation

Over the years, several theories about Tara's fate have been proposed, but none have been definitively proven. Some believe that she was abducted by a local, possibly a truck driver who had been driving through the area at the time. Others speculate that Tara may have been taken by a serial killer who was active in the area during the time of her disappearance.

Some believe that Tara's disappearance is related to the photo that surfaced in 1989. They argue that if Tara was indeed the woman in the photo, then she might have been alive for months or even years after her disappearance. Others have questioned whether the Polaroid photo was a hoax or whether it could have been taken by someone with ulterior motives.

Despite all the theories, the truth about what happened to Tara remains elusive. As of today, no arrests have been made in connection with her disappearance, and the case remains one of New Mexico's most enduring mysteries.

The Impact on the Community

Tara's disappearance has had a profound impact on the local community in Belen and beyond. It has raised awareness about the issue of missing persons and the need for better law enforcement protocols in such cases. Tara's case is often cited as one of the most notable missing persons cases in New Mexico's history.

The Calico family, especially Tara's mother, Patti, has never given up hope of finding answers. Over the years, they have received support from various organizations and individuals who are dedicated to solving missing persons cases. The case remains unsolved, but the Calico family continues to search for closure.

The Legacy of Tara Calico

The mystery of Tara Calico has captivated people for decades. Her disappearance remains unsolved, but it has left a lasting legacy in the world of missing persons cases. Over the years, Tara has become a symbol of the many women who have vanished without a trace, and her case has inspired numerous documentaries, books, and articles.

Though the truth may never be known, Tara's story is a reminder of the fragility of life and the enduring power of hope. Her mother continues to search for answers, and the mystery of Tara's disappearance will likely persist until the day the truth is finally revealed.

Sources

1. "Missing Tara Calico: The Mystery of the Belen Bike Ride" by J. M. Scarbrough, *True Crime Magazine*, 2007.
2. "Tara Calico and the Polaroid Mystery" by S. M. Hernandez, *New Mexico Crime Chronicles*, 1998.
3. "The Disappearance of Tara Calico: The Search for a Missing Girl," *Albuquerque Journal*, 1990.
4. "Missing Persons: A Look at Tara Calico's Case" by M. F. Larson, *Los Angeles Times*, 2004.